HARD TO FAKE

DENVER KODIAKS
BOOK ONE

PIPER LAWSON

Content editing by Becca Mysoor
Line and copy editing by Cassie Robertson
Proofreading by Devon Burke
Cover design by Emily Wittig

For every woman who wants
a good guy with a dirty mouth
to call her Princess

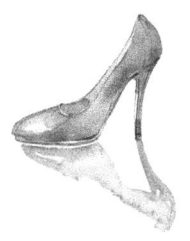

BROOKE

ake it till you make it. Isn't that what they say?

Because if we're not beautiful enough, smart enough, kind enough, capable enough, faceless people will judge us.

We try to be better.

It's easier to pretend.

"More beautiful. More natural. Just... *more, dammit.*" The photographer moves across the wooden planks, his narrowed eyes focused on the camera screen.

I push up the sleeves of my cashmere sweater and follow him.

"This isn't working," Giovanni mutters. A

white man with a narrow face, it's impossible to tell if he's forty or sixty.

"What about like this?" One of the models, Aliya, tilts her head an inch in a pose that's virtually identical to her last one.

We're shooting at the Denver Botanic Gardens. The lily pond is set with stones like gems studding the cold water. In October, many of the blooms have finished for the season, but the green vegetation pops even more against the gray sky.

The models pose at the water's edge, the photographer catching reflections as they sway like flowers in the fall breeze.

Beautiful people in beautiful places doing beautiful things.

"No." Giovanni exhales. "It's the lighting." He gestures to the sun as if he can manipulate it with his hand alone.

We've been trying to make progress for hours, with nothing but dissatisfaction from the photographer. This shoot is for a national magazine, and he's going to be in trouble if he can't produce a killer result.

My eyes latch onto the male model at the front of the group—Chad, or Brad, or Thad. It's been so long since the intros we did this morning, I honestly can't remember.

He's pretty. Harmless.

Boring.

This shoot is going to waste time and money and fall flat if it doesn't have a hook.

The thought sparks something in my brain.

"Movement," I say under my breath.

"What?" Aliya demands. A high-fashion model whose star is on the rise, she has the impatience of someone who's always been told exactly how beautiful she is and thinks she can coast on her razor-sharp cheekbones and flawless skin.

"This place is too peaceful," I say. "Move *bigger*."

I pass my light reflector to another assistant and adjust my shoes. Then I step out in front of the camera onto the first of the rocks.

"Hey! Get back from..." Giovanni trails off.

I tune him out and go farther.

One of my gloves slips out of my pocket, hitting the water's surface. I bend to retrieve it, wobbling as I stick it in my pocket.

I swoop one hand up in the air at a bold angle. Then straddle two stones.

I can't paint the perfect picture, but I trust my

body, my movement.

The photographer watches.

Then starts to click.

The models are giving me curious and affronted looks, as if it's better to sit around not getting the shots the client needs rather than try something new.

"Aliya, can you do that?" the photographer asks, intrigued.

I hear something that sounds like a snort. "You want me to hop on stones like a cracked out rabbit?"

"What's your name?" Giovanni asks, staring straight at me.

"Brooke."

Aliya's cold look can't kill my buzz.

I'm triumphant, basking in my moment of satisfaction. This shoot is saved, the client will be happy, and we can all move on with our lives.

A shrill screech goes up from one of the set assistants stationed near the entrance.

It's a closed set, but a man just entered and is striding over as if he owns it, his height and broad shoulders saying he's used to getting exactly what he wants.

He's big enough to block out part of the sky

and attractive enough no one would mind.

The models get in on the excitement, anticipation sweeping the set like wildfire.

"Is that...?"

"No."

"Oh my God, he's so gorgeous in person."

"And tall. Damn."

Security watches him but with envious smiles rather than suspicion.

What the hell is he doing here?

My weight shifts too far to the right.

Damn it.

I tighten my abs on the opposite side trying to regain my balance.

My foot swipes for the stone but misses.

My arms windmill.

My toe tips into the icy water.

When I dressed for today in my Prada cashmere sweater and pencil skirt and suede Stuart Weitzman ankle booties, I wasn't expecting to pull a Michael Phelps.

Swimming is not in my zone of genius. I look my best dry.

But no matter what prayers I send up to the fashion gods, the water rushes up at me like wall.

The pond is knee deep, but that's hardly a

consolation when I land ass first.

It's shockingly cold, soaking through my tights and bra. I try to swallow my screech but not fast enough.

At the edge of the pond, the models are pointing and gasping.

This time it's at me.

The heat of embarrassment clashes with the numbing cold of the pond.

I wouldn't have fallen in if *someone* hadn't shown up and pulled focus from the entire editorial shoot.

The water ripples in front of me, and a hand appears. I grab it, desperate, and pull myself upright, spitting out a piece of lily pad that got plastered to my mouth.

The hand is attached to a man. One who towers over me now that I'm standing, his athlete's body hard and powerful in jeans and a bomber jacket.

Topping it all off is the most regrettably attractive face I've ever seen. Medium-brown hair with thick brows. A square, smooth-shaven jaw. A wide mouth tipped up at one corner. Eyes that have no business being so goddamned blue.

Excited murmurs go up from the models and

crew. Every person here knows he's world champion Denver Kodiaks shooting guard Miles Garrett. The sexiest man in sports, possibly the world.

Women want him. Guys want to be him.

Sure, he's objectively bangable, with a killer grin, huge hands, and a body that makes you want things you can't say in front of your grandmother.

But he's also Jayden Ellis's righthand man, an extension of the basketball world I've been trying to escape from for years.

"C'mon." His voice is low and amused as he turns, motioning toward his broad back.

He must be joking.

"I'm not riding you like a horse," I scoff, picking a leaf out of my hair.

He grins, the smile of a person who enjoys it and knows he looks good doing it.

I crouch and feel for the bottom of the pond, biting my lip to hold in a whimper as the soggy, frozen cashmere plasters itself to my body.

"What are you doing?" Water soaks up to the knees of his faded-wash jeans.

"I need to find my phone." It was in my skirt pocket, and now it's not.

I bite my lip, swallowing the panic that

wells up.

My life is on that. My work. My world.

The water is dark and opaque, and my foot slips. I keep searching.

On the shore, Giovanni paces. Aliya folds her arms, tapping a toe impatiently.

I take another step, feeling the bottom, and slip on something on the liner of the pool.

"Hurry up. I need to finish this shoot!" the photographer calls.

My would-be rescuer grabs me to keep me from falling. "We stay here any longer, we're going to turn into frogs."

"Only princes turn into frogs, so looks like we're both safe."

My teeth clack together from a sudden shiver that rips through me as the cold water settles into my flesh, my bones.

"Brooke Tamara Ellis." He's suddenly serious. "Your brother's going to kill me if I watch you freeze to death. Get the fuck out of this pond."

I blink at his commanding tone, my chin lifting. "Or else what?"

Before I can respond, he's hoisting me up over his shoulder in a fireman's hold.

He grabs my legs, locking them against his

chest as he straightens to carry me back to shore.

My fingers dig into the muscles of his back.

It's easy to forget how freaking huge he is. Six-four and all of it muscled.

Most of the men I grew up with and went to school with liked to control women with their family name or their trust fund.

This guy literally picked me up and is carrying me through the water as if I weigh nothing.

I don't know what kind of *Princess Bride* shit this is, but I was not prepared. There's a heat starting somewhere deep in my stomach.

Stupid pro athlete.

"Miles!" Aliya rushes up to him when he sets me down on the shore on my feet, her dark hair swinging in a shiny curtain. "I can't believe you did that. What a hero!"

"Do you have a sweater? A blanket?" he asks her, his attention still on me.

"I'm fine," I protest.

"Brock says she's fine, Miles."

"It's Brooke," I start, but I'm distracted by his hands on my upper arms.

"We're almost done here, then I'll be ready to go..." Aliya continues as if I hadn't spoken. There's impatience now and a distracted smile.

I look between them and realize the truth.

He's here for her.

Because he's a massive basketball star and she's a model.

Beautiful people doing beautiful people things.

"It was her own fault," Aliya continues. "She was supposed to be a shoot assistant."

The embarrassment dials up to humiliation.

On my own social media, I'm in front of a camera, contributing to the fantasy life of being a twenty-something without a care in the world except for curating an enviable designer shoe collection and snapping pics of the latest appetizer at a hot new restaurant with my friends.

Today, I was carrying cameras and checking lighting.

My teeth chatter again. "I need to get back to work." I pull out of Miles's grasp and look around for some equipment that needs wrangling.

"You're fired," Giovanni declares. "I cannot have assistants disrupting my shoot."

I wring out the bottom of my sweater, water hitting the deck with a stream of plinks. Indignation edges into my despair.

"Aliya, I need to drive Brooke home," Miles says before I can respond.

"You what?!" We blurt it at the same time.

Aliya's penciled brows drag together as though she's calculating whether she could shove me back in the water and drown me.

I trail him to the parking lot.

"I have a car," I call after him.

"I'll have it dropped off later. Give me your keys."

"No way."

Miles hits the locks and opens the passenger door. "You can drip all over your leather or all over mine."

He's tall enough to easily rest an elbow along the top. His other hand opens, waiting.

I turn it over.

Getting my car detailed was not in my plans for the week.

I drop my keys into his open palm and get in the passenger side.

"You wanted to swim, you could've done it in July rather than the end of October," he suggests as he shifts into the driver's seat.

I pry a piece of curling hair off my forehead. "I had a plan."

"A wet plan?"

So much for the straightening job that took me

an hour.

I'm tempted to toss my hair out of pettiness and watch the droplets spatter his interior, but it would be a crime against the beautiful leather.

"It was going perfectly until you showed up," I inform him.

He snorts and reaches for the vents in front of me, angling them so warm air blows at me.

"Why were you working behind the camera?" he asks.

"Thought I'd broaden my horizons. Learn more about the other side of the industry." I shift in my seat. "What's up with you and Aliya? I didn't know you were dating."

"Wouldn't go that far."

"Ahh, the truth comes out. So, she DM'd you a pic of her topless and you agreed to dinner."

"Or I sent her a pic of me bottomless." He winks and starts to whistle along with the radio.

Miles is the chillest guy I've ever met. Everyone loves him: his teammates, his competition, and every female basketball fan in the country.

But he's not larger than life to me like he is to the rest of the basketball world.

So what if once in a while when his grin lasts too long, it makes my stomach flip?

It's a natural reaction to a hot-AF man. Nothing personal.

"You're not whistling to Kendrick right now," I say.

"The ladies love it."

When he hits the chorus, I can't stop the eye roll.

The heating system starts to send warm air in earnest, and it feels good. I groan and stretch my fingers toward the heat.

Without looking over, Miles turns it up more.

At a light, he reaches into the back seat and retrieves a sweatshirt, dropping it in my lap.

"What size is this, Sasquatch?" I hoist an arm of the giant cotton form into the air.

"I'll find you something else to wear if you tell me why you were really working on that shoot."

My mouth falls open.

Miles's popsicle-chill vibe can lull you into thinking he's safe, but when he cares about something, he'll dig in with a stubbornness even my mom would admire.

Being the only daughter of a United States

senator sounds like a good deal, especially for someone who enjoys being in the spotlight. What you don't realize is that it comes with strings. A lot of them.

Especially in our family.

Be intelligent, but not edgy.

Be polite, but not a pushover.

Be presentable, but conservatively so.

Which, according to my mother, was the cause of her voicemail last week that changed everything.

It's my dirty secret, and I'm not about to share it with anyone, least of all my brother's gorgeous, rich, popular teammate.

I'm already embarrassed, but confessing why I was there would dial that up to off-the-charts humiliation.

"Don't look," I say. I'm not usually self-conscious, but this day has thrown me for a loop.

"Wouldn't dream of it."

With a glance toward Miles to ensure he's watching the road, I peel off the sweater. The warm air feels like heaven on my bare skin as I tug the sweatshirt over my head. It smells clean and a little like Miles. Once I've tugged it down, leaving a pool of fabric around my body, I reach inside to work off my bra.

Who invented these things? I'm half an inch

from to dislocating my shoulder.

A few grunts later, I drop the bra in a soggy pile in my lap.

"You want a medal for that performance?" Miles drawls, navigating traffic.

"It's the least you can do," I retort.

It's not though.

He dragged me out of the pond, got himself soaked in the process, and blew off his date to drive me home.

Miles is one of the good guys.

I shove the shirt sleeves up my arms, feeling like the Michelin man from all the wrinkles.

Miles's gaze flicks over and lands on the stack, my teal lace bra on top. "Lace, huh?"

"Stop it."

He grins, but his attention stays where it is.

"Um. Miles, the light—"

"Shit." He hits the brakes as the yellow switches to red.

I'm tossed forward, the seatbelt lock engaging with a snap across my shoulders.

The last few blocks of the drive pass in silence. Miles pulls up in front of my building without asking for the address.

"Need me to come up to wring your hair out

and tuck you in?"

"No, thank you. You're not the only one with a date tonight," I announce.

I get the briefest satisfaction of seeing his eyes narrow in a very un-Miles way before I get out of the car and slam the door.

"What happened to you?!" Nova gasps as I trip into the café.

I drop into the seat opposite her and fluff my still-damp hair. "A little outdoor swim."

"In October?"

"The pool at the Four Seasons is closed for renovations."

It's Sunday night, and the place is full of decaf-drinking hipsters in mountain chic. This café became Nova's favorite and mine when she lived with me, and it's still not too far from the art studio she rents downtown.

I told Miles I had a date tonight. I didn't say whom it was with.

"This seems like an act of rebellion." My friend pushes a coffee cup matching hers across the table.

Nova is petite and wearing leggings, her hair

tugged up in a ponytail that brushes her shoulders. We're the same age but she seems younger, probably thanks to the big blue eyes that reveal exactly what she's feeling at any moment.

"Not even. I was assisting on this editorial shoot, but they were too narrow-minded for my ideas."

She frowns. "Assisting," she echoes. "You were helping with a shoot instead of being at the center of it? What's going on?"

When Miles asked me, I couldn't imagine sharing the truth with him, especially because he'd turn around and tell my brother.

But Nova's discreet and the kind of friend who makes you want to let your guard down. I've never once felt judged or less than.

"I'm broke," I say bluntly.

Her gaze drops to my designer outfit before lifting again. "Back up. Explain."

"My mom's always helped with... you know."

"Money," she supplies with a nod.

"Yup. It made sense. After high school, I would have been happy to go to a junior college, but she wanted me to go to this expensive private school, pledge a traditional sorority, fit the image of a senator's daughter. I told her I didn't need all of that or the debt that went with it. So, to convince me, she said she'd help."

"Okay."

"Well, after graduation, I guess she decided my image was important to her politically and didn't want me living on ramen with four roommates. So, she kept helping." I inspect my nails for damage. No casualties from my little *Swan Lake* impression earlier. "For the last three years, she's helped... until last week. She decided to stop."

"Why?"

I lift a shoulder. "Her polling team saw a post on my social that showed nine percent too much side boob for her constituents."

As one of a handful of Black female senators, my mom feels a lot of pressure to lead by example. She's nearing the end of her second term and coming up on reelection.

The thing is, if Mom had asked me herself to take down a picture, I would have done it.

Probably.

Maybe.

I started building my social media back in college with what society would now call fashion and lifestyle content, though I never thought of it that way. To me, it was just me living my life.

A styled, curated life.

It was as genuine as it could be with the addition of thoughtful outfits, lighting, and captions. But lately, my mom has been more concerned about what I post and say, which might not be a problem except that I've gotten less concerned.

I post hiking pics, moments on the street that make me pause and think, blurry nights out with my friends.

When someone comes at me on the internet, I stick up for myself. I used to turn a blind eye, but over the past year, the level of nitpicking has gone through the roof—on everything from my appearance to my activities to the people I spend my time with.

If it was confined to me, I could take it. But strangers pick at other women for how they look or act and it makes me angry.

Not everyone can handle the weight of that criticism.

They shouldn't have to.

In my head, I play back the voicemail from my mom. Phrases like "can't afford mistakes" and "I won't be covering for you again" come to mind.

It's less a stinging hurt than a constant twinge,

like when I pulled a muscle the first day of dance camp as a kid and ignored it for the rest of the week.

My friend twists a piece of blond-and-pink hair around her finger. "Are you going to be okay?"

Nova's parents died when she was in school, and she had to figure things out on her own. She's resourceful, and I'm determined to be too.

My brother would laugh if I told him I'm broke. We're two years and six months apart in age, and he's a professional basketball player who makes an insane amount of money—the kind that means you could buy a different house every season.

"Totally. Though I do need a new phone." I reach into my bag and pull out the geriatric one I found in a drawer. It won't update, and I can barely log in to my socials. It's going to be a nightmare to post until I can get a new one, but I never appreciated how much they cost before.

"What are you going to do?" Nova prods.

That is the question.

I have a handful of brand partnerships, though those mostly provide me merch in exchange for promotions rather than cash.

I briefly scanned job openings online, but

everything required a specific degree or technical skills I don't have. The ones I qualify for don't pay what I need.

A new post pops up at the top of my feed from an account that I follow.

"One of the alums from my sorority runs this big fashion brand," I explain to Nova. "She's crushing it, and she's always built her brand by supporting other women." I swipe through the posts, impressed.

They have a new collection launching soon. It's a different vibe than the last one, emphasizing natural fabrics in bold colors.

Nova reads the post with me. "Does she need spokesmodels or brand partners? You should put your name in."

I turn the idea over, tapping a finger against my lip. My friend is right that it could be a perfect fit for me. "She's a big deal."

"So are you," Nova says loyally. "Have you seen how many followers you have? Plus, you're smart, warm, and people want to be around you."

My chest squeezes as I reach for my drink. "You're the best. You know that, right?"

She beams. "Okay, speaking of fashion... please

tell me you're still going to the Kodiaks Halloween party this week."

"I need to make sure my brother is a good host."

Last year, the annual Halloween party was hosted by an ex-player who was the cause of endless team grief and drama. I told Jay he needed to host this year's party to erase that from everyone's mind.

"What are you going as?"

I navigate my phone, grimacing as I wait for it to load my reference picture.

"That's wholesome," she comments once I show her.

"Not the way I'm doing it."

She laughs appreciatively. "I heard the prize is a thousand dollars."

My interest perks up. If I won, that would get me a new phone.

My old one buzzes with a notification.

Miles: Wanted to make sure you didn't fall into the bathtub before your date.

Brooke: Why are you texting me? I lost my phone.

Miles: But you're responding so... ;)

My lips curve.

On my way over here, I passed a bus stop with a picture of the starting lineup of the World Champion Denver Kodiaks.

Standing in the middle was Miles, a basketball gripped between his massive palms, his purple jersey revealing muscled arms. He was facing down the camera with a smirk that could melt a woman's panties off.

He was always a fan favorite, but after the playoffs, he became even more popular. Now that their season has officially started, excitement and expectations are off the charts.

The whole city, the entire *state*, has had a collective hard-on for the Kodiaks since they won the championship last year.

"Who's that?" Nova asks, curious.

"Miles drove me home after the shoot. He was

there to pick up one of the models. He left with me instead."

"Fascinating." Nova shifts forward, her dark lashes fluttering. "Why would he do that?"

"Because my brother would have Miles's ass if he let me drown?" I supply. "Hint all you want, but we are never getting together." I set down the phone firmly.

"But you have chemistry."

"I don't date basketball players."

"Who do you date? Because as long as we've known each other, I haven't seen you date anyone for more than a few weeks."

I kick her lightly with my toe under the table in retaliation.

"Shacking up with some baller from my brother's team is the last thing I need."

I grew up under my mom's public persona, and now I have to deal with my brother's. He's one of the top point guards in the NBA, and even when I try to live on my own terms, existing in the same city means his world collides with mine more often than not.

"I hooked up with one of the guys on my brother-in-law's team. It worked out pretty well," Nova says with an innocent smile.

"And he's the lucky one, Mrs. Wade," I say, my attention falling to her gigantic diamond ring, now with a matching wedding band thanks to Clayton Wade, the Kodiaks' all-star forward and Nova's husband.

She didn't know who Clay was when they met. It was a very sexy case of mistaken identity, and I was here for it.

"So, Miles doesn't even get a chance?" she pleads.

The way he carried me out of the water comes back, coupled with the lingering look in the car after I changed in the passenger seat.

I don't think about him like that.

Okay, sometimes I think about him like that.

But even if Miles decided tomorrow that chasing Kodashians is inferior to dating a woman who actually sees who he is and challenges him, hooking up with the most popular player in the NBA who's also my brother's teammate would be a kind of complicated I avoid.

"I will never date the golden boy." I click into my social account, relieved to see the number of comments piling up on my latest post. "There's only so much sun to go around, and I die in the shadows."

2

MILES

LAST YEARS' CHAMPION KODIAKS A "ONE-HIT WONDER"? *HOOPS NEWS* HAS THE SCOOP

"Come on, man. We're late. Coach is going to have your ass," I say.

Waffles whines up at me from the pavement, his big, dark eyes taking over his tiny, squished face.

"We agreed to this. We shook on it. Now you're acting like it never happened?"

I'm already behind, as the buzzing alert on my

phone has let me know twice.

French Bulldogs are equal parts muscle and cute. I tug the leash and he braces against me, shifting his ass as if he can glue it to the pavement.

Thirty-pound professional napper vs twenty pro athlete.

It's obvious to everyone but Waffles which way this is going to go.

"Don't make me do it," I warn.

I adjust my bag across my shoulder and scoop the Frenchie into my arms. In the three years I've had him, he still doesn't love me picking him up. His whimper reminds me his life is balls as I walk with him toward the doors.

"Miles!" a female voice calls from behind me.

I turn to see three twenty-something women waving and smiling.

"Great game against Boston the other night," a blonde woman says, making her way toward me.

I nod since both my hands are full. "Thanks, I appreciate that."

We got a win, and my shooting line was impeccable.

"I'm a huge fan. Can I get a picture?" she stops in front of me, breathless.

Posing with fans is something I have no

problem with. I get that some athletes prefer their privacy, but they're in the wrong business. Being available to take a picture is the least I can do for all the time and money they spend to cheer us on.

"What a cute dog."

Waffles makes a little grunt in his throat, and I shoot him a look before shifting him to my other side away from her.

She presses as close as possible to take the selfie.

"Right. Well, it was nice to meet you. I'll see you around?" Her smile is hopeful, like she wants me to ask for her number.

"You got it," I reply easily. Not because I think I'll see her, but because it's the best thing to say to fans.

I have a healthy confidence—some might say cockiness—but it still throws me how much interest I get from women. The dark hair and the straight teeth courtesy of braces always did me right, but since we won, it's like I look too long and panties drop.

Most days, I'm into it.

I'm the guy you have fun with for a night, a week, a summer. I can put a smile on anyone's face, and when it comes to women, I'll give them a memory they can look back on fondly.

I'm not looking for a deep connection.

Except since we became world champs, the number of people who want something from me has grown exponentially.

I dropped math first year of college, so I'm not sure how many that is, but it's a lot.

"That *Hoops News* article is BS!" she calls after me.

I frown as I adjust the dog in my arms. "Nice to meet you too," I reply even though I didn't get her name.

I'm a professional basketball player. Been wanting to be one since I was old enough to score my first basket.

It's a dream job.

It's also a roller coaster. I live for the highs, try not to let the lows drag me down, because the highs arc really fucking high.

Winning championships. Making millions. Fans everywhere I go.

The lows?

I promised myself I wouldn't think about those anymore.

I check my phone for a response to the message I sent first thing this morning.

Miles: Haven't talked in a couple days. All good?

Miles: Gonna stop by after practice if I don't hear back.

Concern edges into my gut.

"What's the little dude doing here?" Rookie is lacing up his sneakers when I get to the court and set down my gear bag, open at the top with my dog inside.

"Been in a funk for the past week. Figured he'd be better here where I can keep an eye on him than at home. He'll be quiet," I tell our coach, who narrows his eyes before nodding toward the banner hanging from the rafters.

Denver Kodiaks.

World Champions.

We got the banner for the first game of this season, and it's like a god watching over us. The kind that looks out for us but has expectations too.

"Put that shit away," Clay says to our point guard Jay, who's looking at his phone.

"What?" I ask.

"This *Hoops News* article," Jay grumbles. "Saying we were lucky last year, not good."

As our leader, Jay's pissed. It's my job to take the edge off.

I clap a hand on his shoulder. "No one wins a world championship on luck, but having a little doesn't hurt."

"You know the hardest thing in this league?" Coach asks after calling the team to order. "Not winning a championship, winning a second one."

"Winning the first one wasn't the easiest either," Rookie says under his breath.

"Damn straight, Rookie," one of our bench guys says.

"You can't keep calling me that."

"Sure we can. Technically, you're still on your rookie contract, right? Just second-year," Darius, the backup point guard we picked up in the off-season, points out.

Rookie frowns. "Stay out of it, new guy. Want me to call you 'new guy' all year?"

"If you want—"

Jay clears his throat, ignoring the others. "The

first three games of the season showed us we're stronger than ever."

"Strong?" Heads turn back to Coach. "We stole the win from LA, and we got out of Boston thanks to a few calls that went our way."

Tension rolls through the room.

"Where's Atlas?" I'm looking around. Our center was injured in a hard hit the first game of the season, but he was supposed to be back today.

Coach huffs out a breath. "He's day to day."

Normally, we're a loud bunch. There's a lot of laughing, teasing, calling each other out on our bullshit.

Now silence falls over us.

"Meaning...?" Jay asks.

"Meaning we're a man down for a game or two."

A gloom descends over the gym.

It's true that this year there's a target on our backs. If what happened to Atlas is any indication, no one in either conference is pulling any punches.

"It's a couple of games. We'll hold the fort," I say with confidence.

I'm a role player, the guy who can slot in anywhere. I love the game almost as much as I love getting to joke and catch up with my guys from around the league.

I keep us level when the world tries to rip us off our axis.

The higher you fly, the more important that is.

My phone buzzes in my bag.

The name on the screen coupled with the message have me intrigued instantly.

Brooke: I need your dog.

Most girls show up in my phone to ask me out or send me naked pics. Not this one.

Miles: You want to cast him in a production, you have to go through his talent agent.

Brooke: He goes with my costume for the party, and I intend to win.

"You put her up to this?" I ask Waffles.

He cocks his head, his dark eyes becoming hypnotic pools of cuteness overload.

Brooke's not so much a woman as a force of

nature. She's brave and bold and unapologetic, which lands her in hot water—or yesterday, cold water.

I'd never tell her how much I enjoyed carrying her out of the pond, because she'd cut off my balls and nail them to her door like jingle bells.

I would've driven most girls home after what happened because it was the right thing to do, but this wasn't just any girl—it was Brooke.

Brooke, who'd show up for a backyard BBQ in head-to-toe Fendi carrying a bag of hot dog buns.

Who makes fun of my practical jokes but can come up with a mean prank herself.

Who'll stomp her spiked heels and tell off any of the guys as though she's one of them.

Who'd probably die before sliding into my DMs with a naked pic.

Not that I wouldn't take a long look if she did.

From the gangly freshman I met back when Jay and I were still playing college ball, she's grown up to be a damned smoke show.

But she's sister to the guy who's my teammate, my friend. She's so far off-limits she might as well live on the moon.

I'm definitely not still thinking about how it

felt to have her over my shoulder, my palm across the back of her thighs.

Jay asks, "What're you going to the party as? There's an epic prize." He grins. "Brooke's been working on her costume for weeks."

The guys keep talking costumes, but I'm curious. I type out a text.

Miles: Tell me the concept. Waffles's management needs to approve it.

Brooke: Tell Waffles's management it's top secret.

Miles: Then he gets half the prize winnings.

Brooke: Twenty-five percent.

Miles: Should be an even partnership.

Brooke: Not when he doesn't have to wear heels.

I chuckle and tuck the phone away.

She's always been more than other girls, even in college.

Funnier.

Braver.

More caring.

In another world, Brooke and I would make a hell of a team.

Rescuing her was even worth getting chewed out by Aliya on voicemail for bailing. I had my assistant send her flowers as an apology, but I'm regretting it because she's texted me half a dozen times since.

The first time we hung out, we agreed neither of us was looking for serious, but it's starting to feel as if she wants more than I have to give. I don't tell women I'm unavailable to play hard to get or because I want to be noncommittal.

It's because the only long-lasting relationships I have are with my guys and my dog. I'm protective as hell about the people I choose, and I don't let just anyone in.

When I tune back in, Jay's scrubbing a towel across his face. "You think I can't organize a costume party?"

"You totally hired it out," Rookie tosses.

I brighten at that piece of information. "Least we know it's going to be good."

"Come on." Jay looks hurt.

"You couldn't choose the signature drink," Clay says.

Jay stares at him, his eyes cool and his face unreadable. "Just for that, I'm awarding you a penalty."

"The hell kind of costume contest has penalties?!" I demand.

"The kind I came up with."

My phone dings with a notification. I glance down, hoping it's the person I'm still waiting to hear from after an entire day.

Instead, it's Aliya saying next time she wants different flowers.

I silence the phone.

"Well, you heard Coach." I hook an elbow around Jay's neck and the other around Clay. "Only thing harder than winning once is running it back. Better get to work."

These guys are my family. Whether we're winning or not, that won't change.

It can't.

3

BROOKE

KODIAKS DROP EARLY SEASON GAME TO MIAMI. IS THIS THE START OF THE DOWN SLIDE? *HOOPS NEWS* HAS THE SCOOP.

Brooke: Shower and get your sorry asses through media. We're going out.

Jay: Did you see the L? Last thing we need is a club night.

Clay: I'm hitting the gym.

Brooke: Come on, Chloe. Back me up.

Chloe: It's not the worst idea.

Chloe: (That's off the record. As a friend, not in my official capacity as Kodiaks head of PR.)

Jay: Obvs. It's the BearFam chat, not the management chat.

Rookie: You're only in here because Jay used to bang you.

Chloe: 1. I am a member of the Kodiaks organization, and you're a second-year rookie, so I pull rank.
2. *I* used to bang *Jayden*. Not the other way around.

Rookie: I'm so in love right now.

Brooke: Finish your workout, shower off your gross AF selves, and get downtown.

Jay: No club. We'll meet up at Mile High.

～

The Kodiaks loss is all over the news.

It's a blow, but the team is taking it extra hard for so early in the season. They're champions, and everyone expects them to win, including themselves.

The game looked like a close one, and I hate seeing my brother in a bad mood. Plus, I want a night off from thinking about my own problems.

Earlier today, I opened my laptop computer to look at my bank account for the first time in a while. It couldn't be that bad. I'd probably saved a lot. Maybe I could get by for a year without my mom topping me up.

My stomach sank as I read through the numbers.

Without my mom's help, I'd run out of money in less than thirty days.

I'd closed the tab and opened a new one, searching for information on my sorority sister Elise's brand.

She's a visionary. Her company makes clothes that are high end but insanely wearable and at price points more women can afford. They've expanded internationally at an unprecedented pace since Elise graduated two years ahead of me. Rumor has it she declined an offer to sell her business for five hundred million last year.

I love fashion. It's my decoration and my armor.

Nova is a super talented artist, but it's hard to carry a painting with you when you get on a plane or even through a tough day.

Almost anyone would say that I'm aiming high by trying to forge a partnership, but since Nova mentioned it, the idea won't leave.

I researched whom Elise used to promote the brand in the past, what influencers have been wearing her clothing in their posts. While I was doing that, I found Elise herself tagged in another sister's post.

The caption on Caroline's photo, one where she's embracing Elise, reads: *Can't wait to see my favorite sisters next weekend!*

Our former chapter president made every overachiever in the sorority look like a slacker. She took the same etiquette classes I did but actually enjoyed them. Her social media is impeccable, every post with full makeup and not a blonde hair out of place.

In other words...

She's exactly the type of influencer Elise would align herself with.

I dig an Alexander McQueen cocktail dress out of my closet and put it on with silver heels. Nova's out of town for a gallery show, but at least Chloe's in.

Mile High is the team's unofficial bar. Nova's husband, Clay, has been a part owner almost since the time he joined the Kodiaks.

The walls are papered with images of the team from over the years, newspaper articles, plus collector's items like signed hats and jerseys under glass. Every starting player has a drink named after him.

It's a casual spot where the team can sit alongside fans.

Right now, the place is just under capacity, probably owing to the midweek loss.

"Why's everyone so freaked after a loss? It's early," I ask my brother.

"There are articles calling us one-hit wonders."

"Show them you're not."

The entire starting line-up promised to come out, which is an accomplishment.

Clay will bail soon, heading home to whatever hundred-step conditioning routine over-thirty all-stars do to stay in shape. Rookie is chatting with Chloe. I haven't seen Miles yet.

So, I have a moment alone with Jay.

"Unless you believe it too," I prompt at his silence.

"Course not. But there's no doubt we have a target on our backs." He grimaces. "Last year, no one saw us coming. This year, they're rolling out the welcome mat."

Sierra slides us over drinks and my brother thanks her.

"But now you know you can do it," I counter. "That's better than most guys in the league can say."

"You're a good hype woman," Jay says with a grin.

I raise a brow. "You're just now realizing this?"

My attention cuts to the guys. Rookie's laughing with Chloe. "They look cute."

Jay pushes his drink back across the bar like he's thought twice, reaching for a water instead. "Come on. You know it's complicated between us."

"Because she's your ex. So she's not allowed to date any of your teammates, ever?"

"Hell no," he insists. "Keep the drama out of the locker room. Family is family."

"Wait. Chloe's family or the team is?"

"Both."

"Whatever you say, big brother." I pat him on the arm and head for the bathroom.

On my way, I spot a woman bent over double by the door. I pull up sharply.

"Are you okay?"

"Fine." She's breathing normally, but her eyes are hazy.

I get her into the bathroom and hold her hair while she throws up twice.

"I swear I'm not that drunk, it's just been a weird day," she groans as she straightens.

"Don't sweat it. I'm Brooke."

"Lori." She smiles weakly as we head out of the bathroom. "I'm here with my boyfriend, but we had a fight." She nods toward a guy at one of the booths with blond hair and a flipped collar. He's gripping an empty highball glass and surrounded by a few others, including some women he's grinning at. "He's not supposed to be drinking—he promised me he wouldn't, because it's not good when he does —but he's already started. The thing is, he makes me feel like I'm the crazy one, and..." Her cheeks flush. "Sorry, I don't need to dump this on you."

"It's okay. Don't let him gaslight you."

"Speaking from experience, huh?" She nods, not waiting for me to respond. "I think I'm going to go home."

I walk outside with her and call an Uber on my account. She thanks me again as I put her inside the car.

"What did you do with my girlfriend?" a voice demands from behind me.

When I turn, I find myself toe to toe with the guy she pointed out earlier. "I helped her get home," I say evenly.

"I say when it's time to leave." His eyes narrow, an ugly sneer on his face.

"Actually, she's a grown woman who gets to decide things for herself, like when to leave and with whom."

He mutters something under his breath that has my brows lifting.

It's not until he shoves my shoulder, hard enough that I trip into the brick wall behind me, that I realize he could be more trouble than I thought.

A massive body shifts between us.

"You like your hands?" Miles's voice is friendly.

"What?"

I can't see Boyfriend-of-the-Year's expression, but he sounds confused, irritated, and definitely more alert than he was a moment ago.

"I asked if you like your hands. Because if you want to keep them, you won't touch her again."

The other guy was clearly thinking of picking a fight, but when he sizes up exactly whom he's dealing with, he changes his mind.

"Good plan," I can't resist calling around Miles's shoulder as the other man slinks away.

My pulse pounds in my veins as I realize how close I came to getting injured. A twinge in my knuckles makes me look down to see a red scratch.

"You're hurt," Miles says as he turns, his bomber jacket brushing my arm.

"It's only a scrape. I'll rinse it off when I get home." I wave him off. "You get worse every day on the court."

"We're not talking about me."

He reaches into the pocket of his jeans for his

wallet.

"You're not fixing my scratch with a condom," I protest, but he produces a Band-Aid.

Miles unwraps the strip and puts it carefully over the scrape, then swipes a thumb along my wrist. Warmth rushes along my skin.

"What would you have done if he didn't back down?" I ask, glancing over my shoulder as we return to the bar. "You're an NBA player. The golden boy, no less. You can't hit a stranger in a bar."

In my experience, Miles Garrett would sooner buy another guy a beer than threaten him.

"And you learned this because...?"

"You took me for pancakes once back in college."

The year he and my brother got drafted to the NBA, Miles did pre-season prep at a minor league team close to my school. He dropped in more than a few times, mostly when Jay was around too, but one time he took me for breakfast.

"We snuck out around all the sorority sisters who organized Sunday morning runs," I prompt when he doesn't respond. "You picked me up and insisted on paying with all your rookie contract money."

"Well, thank fuck I've gotten a raise since then." Miles reaches for his wallet, and I wave him off.

"This one's on me." I buy the next round for both of us and take a sip of my cocktail. "I'm glad it was you out there tonight and not my brother."

"Just at the right place at the right time." He reaches for his drink, his huge hand swallowing up the glass. "Why not Jay?"

"He'd tell me not to be reckless. Most people give me shit for not thinking before I act."

Miles surveys me, a slow look top to bottom. "Think I like you better when you don't."

A hum of electricity darts through me as he lifts his glass in a silent toast, then presses it to his lips. His throat throbs as he swallows.

Nearby, a group of Kodashians in a booth watch with envy. Each one of them would kill to be where I'm standing right now.

"Thanks."

"For having your back?" Miles leans an elbow on the bar.

"No. For saying that."

On impulse, I press up to kiss his cheek, catching his startled expression before I grab Chloe to come dance with me.

4

BROOKE

To: belliso3@alumni.cc.edu
From: kappapastpresident@alumni.cc.edu
Subject: Reunion updates!

Dear Kappa Sister,

The big reunion is two weeks away! I hope you're as excited as we are to see so many familiar faces.

If you're receiving this email, it means we have incomplete fields in your registration.

Please review your submission to ensure a smooth weekend for all.

Your committee chair and past president,

Caroline

"*D*amn, you look good." Rookie gives me a once-over at the door.

The sky blue fabric of my dress scoops at the front, flares from my waist and ends midway down my thighs.

I twist a strand of my hair, tied in two pig tails, around a finger. "You know who I am?"

"French maid."

"Nice try."

There are at least fifty people here, mostly Kodiaks players and staff and plus-ones. I checked in with the guy Jay hired to run the gate.

Normally, I'd get ready with Nova, but since she and Clay are doing a couple's costume, she said she was needed at home. So, I put mine together myself, right down to the sparkly red Louboutins.

Tonight, my goal is to win the costume contest so I can buy a new phone. Jay didn't tell me who's judging, so I need to make sure I'm seen everywhere.

"Sexy nurse?" Rookie tries again.

"I'm Dorothy. From *The Wizard of Oz.*"

"Is that like *Real Housewives*?"

"Back off my sister." Jay appears from nowhere. "You hit on her, you'll be riding the bench for the rest of the year."

Rookie grins. "Might be worth it."

"Keep dreaming," I counter sweetly.

The front of Jay's place is decorated like a haunted house. Music pulses from inside, the party beckoning.

"You boys enjoy your pissing contest. I'm going in," I say.

I start in through the haunted house, but Jay follows.

My brother's house is a historic property. When I saw it from a realtor I follow online over the summer, I knew someone had to buy it and put their love—and money—into it.

Jay's been watching home renovation shows in his downtime and decided he's going to do an overhaul this season.

"You shouldn't worry about me," I remind him as I walk beneath fake cobwebs.

He's six inches taller and has to duck to avoid

getting them across the face. "Can't help it. You're my little sis."

Spooky laughter streams from the corner, and Jay jumps.

"You're scared of your own party?" I tease him. "Save that worry for your season."

"Thought you wanted us to stop worrying."

"Atlas is still out, right?" I ask.

"He's day to day. He'll be back in no time."

We make our way through a hall of mirrors. A plastic bat swings from the ceiling, and my brother hollers, jumping onto my foot.

"Hey! These shoes are expensive," I protest.

We trip out of the hallway and into the great room where the music is pounding.

Lights swirl from a corner, casting the room in blue.

There's a solid crowd and everyone is in costume. Attractive people grace the couches, stand in the kitchen, and laugh in groups in the corners.

My gaze lands on Nova standing next to the massive marble island. She waves, and I start for her, but my ankle rolls. I bend to check my shoes. *Dammit.* The heel on my Louboutins cracked when Jay tripped over me. It's still attached but barely, and I can't put all my weight on it.

I shuffle over to my friend.

"Hey, beautiful!" Nova beams. She's wearing a long blond wig that cascades down her back with a crown on her head.

"Princess Peach," I decide, and she claps. "Oh my God, tell me Clay is Mario and has a little moustache."

My friend winks. "Come on, let's get drinks."

Chloe's in the kitchen, plus Sierra, the bartender from Mile High, who's a friend of the team. Music is pumping, and I survey the room with a smile. It's a great vibe.

"I need you to sample these new drinks," Sierra calls over the music. "You want a slam dunk or a rim runner?"

I arch a brow as I take one from her at random and toss it back. "It's good."

Sierra's long dark hair sways as she moves. Her burgundy lips that match her leather pants.

"This look is fierce," I say, waving a finger at her outfit.

"Better be. I need to get laid tonight because I can't get these pants off myself."

I set the glass on the counter and scan the room. The costumes are strong, and I want to win.

Our bartender friend pours another round of shots for a pair of guys who've come up.

"Looking good, Sierra," one of them comments.

She gives them a once-over. "Come find me at two."

"Which one of us?" They exchange a surprised look.

"Didn't hear me specify."

They walk away giggling like middle school girls, high-fiving as they disappear into the crowd.

"You ever had a threesome?" Sierra asks.

"I don't think I could fit another guy in my bed besides Clay," Nova admits.

Sierra fixes another round for someone who flagged her down, her hands flying from one bottle to another. "It's like Tetris. You'd be surprised how much room there is when you're not sleeping."

I snort. "Logistics is the least of your concerns. The fact that Clay would rip the head off any guy who looks at you too long is a bigger problem."

The song changes, and the music seems to get louder.

My phone buzzes.

It's Ruby messaging me a photo from the sorority's account.

Without looking at it, I type back, trying my best to ignore the crack in the screen.

Brooke: Can't believe you have time to scroll social, Mrs. Doctor.

Ruby: I'll always be your Big Sis. Did you see who Caroline's bringing as her date next weekend?

I start to type that I don't give a damn who the sorority sister who always rubbed me the wrong way is going with, even if she's decided to be Elise's new BFF.

Just for the hell of it, I click on the picture.

Half a dozen smiling faces greet me, including Caroline's and those of a couple sisters I recognize.

The other three are guys, presumably their significant others.

Two are strangers, but the third is instantly familiar.

My happy buzz disintegrates.

Blond hair. Perfect smile. Tom Ford polo.

An unpleasant tsunami of emotions crashes into me.

"Unbelievable," I mutter.

"What's wrong?" Nova asks.

"One of my sorority sisters is bringing my ex to this reunion."

Sierra asks, "How big an ex are we talking?"

The floor spins and I'm not drunk enough to blame the alcohol.

Not yet, anyway.

"We grew up together. He was my first everything, and his family was a big donor to my mom's campaign."

"So, things ended on good terms?" Sierra guesses.

I reach across the island for a liquor bottle, pour some into a shot glass, and toss it back.

"I'll take that as a no." Sierra holds the bottle away before I can pour another. "Who are *you* taking to the event?"

"I was planning to go solo."

"You still can," Nova insists.

The idea of showing up and staying confident and resolute and convincing my sorority sis I can rep her brand better than Caroline while she has Kevin at her side, making her look good and making me insecure in front of Elise…

No, thank you.

I mentally run through the guys on my phone I could rope into a semi-romantic weekend in Vail. Plenty of successful, attractive men.

They all have baggage.

If I bring someone random, it will seem opportunistic, like I'm motivated by jealousy or competitiveness.

I take another shot.

I've had enough rim runners when Clay comes up behind Nova, snuggling her. "Hey, Pink."

"Tonight, it's Peach," she reminds him.

"Where's your moustache?" I call.

He reaches a tattooed hand into a pocket and produces a dark, curled chunk of hair. "Kept getting stuck up my nose."

Seeing them together, how Clay's grumpy expression brightens when he sees Nova and the way she comes alive around him, is really sweet.

With the alcohol buzzing through my system, I can admit my pride isn't the only reason I'm in a mood over my ex attending this Kappa reunion.

"You seen my dog?" I ask, irritated.

Nova points, and my gaze lands on Miles.

He's so hot it's like a gut punch.

His dark hair curls around his ears. He stands out even in a room full of athletes, his relaxed grace beyond sexy because it's entirely natural.

"Who's the Kodashian?" Nova asks. Now that I look, he's talking to a familiar woman in a black catsuit that probably takes longer to get off than it did to get on.

"Aliya. She was at the shoot the other day."

"She's come to the bar before," Sierra weighs in. "She's a snob and a terrible tipper."

I'm surprised he'd bring her here... and a little disappointed, especially when he said they were only hooking up.

Not that I spend time thinking about the kind of woman Miles should be with. But obviously, if she's more than some Kodashian, she should be smart, and fun, and enough of a ball-buster to challenge him.

I put my fingers to my lips and whistle. Heads swivel to face me, a few people covering their ears.

Moments later, Waffles races through the crowd, jumping excitedly to plant his sturdy paws on my legs.

"Hey, handsome!" I say, bending to scratch his cute little ears.

He's nothing like Toto, but he's perfect. We never had a dog growing up, but I wish we had.

Waffles and I are still having our lovefest when a set of feet—human and enormous—stop in front of me. I do my best to straighten, which is hard while being half drunk with a broken heel.

My reward is pure male hotness in the form of long legs, a wide torso, and a handsome face.

Miles is wearing camouflage pants and a faux fur vest with nothing beneath it, his hair swept back off his face in a way that makes his nose and jaw even sharper. In the low light, it's impossible to see the warmth in his blue eyes, but I feel it penetrate my skin.

Miles's gaze flicks over me, lingering on my legs. "Dorothy with daddy issues?"

"Haha." I nod to the plastic axe hanging from his belt. "Are you Rambo?"

"Mountain Ken." He tosses his hair back.

Someone hollers for Clay, and the big, tattooed man looks up.

"I'll be back." He brushes his lips over Nova's. It's sweet and sexy.

I'm the least romantic woman in the world, but even I have to bite my cheek to keep from sighing.

Someone passes by with Jell-O shots, and I grab two.

"Why thank you." Miles takes one from me, our skin brushing.

"They were both for me," I grumble.

We clink glasses and toss back our drinks.

The music changes, and Nova makes a dash for the floor. "I need to dance to this. Catch you guys in a second."

I watch her weave through the crowd, meeting up with Clay. He drags her against him.

"No one should be that cute," I say.

"Almost makes you believe in love," he agrees.

"Do you? Believe in love?"

He turns over my question. "Love is about respect. Friendship is love. Family is love. Mutually beneficial banging, like *really* good fucking, well, that's a kind of love too. And maybe there's something more than all of that."

I survey him with new appreciation. He's objectively gorgeous. His blue eyes stare straight into your soul. His big hands make you wonder what they'd feel like on your body. He's got the kind of confidence that puts other people at ease.

Sure, Miles is always smack in the middle of every joke or prank, but in that way where even if he's everywhere and loud and laughing, he somehow leaves you wanting more.

He's the kind of guy any girl would love to have on her arm at a party.

Or a reunion.

I'm remembering how he had my back the other night at Mile High, no questions asked.

"Most people give me shit for not thinking before I act."

"I like you better when you don't."

Alcohol buzzes through my veins, whispering seductive promises to my brain.

"Hey, Miles, if I asked you to do something crazy for me, would you do it?" The voice is far away but sounds like mine.

"Are we talking felony or misdemeanor?" Miles's brow lifts, and he looks even more charmingly wicked.

There are bad ideas and then there are Bad Ideas. The kind that you regret for years.

If I was sober, I'd recognize which one this was.

As it stands, I blame the booze burning my throat, the ugly surprise over Caroline parading around my ex at the reunion, and the dazzling veneer that is Miles Garrett, shining like a six-pack-boasting mirage I can practically taste.

"Take me to Vail for the weekend," I call over the music. "Act like you're obsessed with me."

His smile freezes.

"There's a sorority reunion and I need a date," I add. *Probably should have led with that.* "Not a real date. Just a fake one."

Finally, he blinks. "And you're asking me because...?"

I tap my lip. "I'm drunk and you'll go out with anyone."

"That's what you think of my standards," he scoffs.

"That's what I *know* of your standards."

Miles covers his heart with a hand as if my words are a bullet ripping through him. "I'll have you know I have enjoyed the company of some upstanding women."

"You've 'enjoyed' so many that it would be hard not to."

He grins, a genuine intrigue on his face as he studies me. Like he's never really seen me before.

"There you are!" Aliya comes up with a smile that's only for him. "I know you've been looking everywhere for me."

Her catsuit looks painted on, and she beams as her hand finds Miles's bicep. Her appearance and possessiveness hit me like the icy water from the garden pond.

My eyes roll so hard it's a wonder they don't get stuck. "Hi, Aliya." I waggle my fingers.

"Have we met?"

"Yeah. It's Brooke."

"Right. Brock."

"She said Brooke," Miles repeats, and Aliya turns her attention to him.

"Oh, okay. And what's my name?" Her voice is teasing.

"Aliya."

"Just checking."

She's draped over him like a second skin.

"Forget what I asked. I'm drunk." I glance at the Frenchie sitting obediently at my heels. "Let's go, Waffles. We need to find the judges and make ourselves known."

I'm gone before Miles can respond or make me feel like more of an idiot.

5

MILES

"Scary is where it's at," Atlas calls over the music, lifting his Frankenstein arms.

"No. Sexy gets you laid," Rookie counters.

Jay shakes his head, holding up a hand. "Halloween is for girls to dress sexy."

"But if they're going to put the effort in, least you can do is show them what's in it for them," I point out, patting my abs.

Rookie high-fives me.

"Nice fur coat," Atlas says.

"It's a vest," I tell him.

"Rambo?" Rookie guesses.

"Mountain Ken." I hold up my axe.

The kitchen is full of people drinking and

laughing. It's easy to pick out the players and former players in any basketball mixer because we're head and shoulders above the crowd.

"You drink anything that's not mint tea or some kind of rehab concoction, you're gonna hear about it." Jay stabs a finger at Atlas as our big guy reaches for a beer.

Today, we had team meetings and practice. I stayed late for an extra-long workout and to watch tape, trying to study sequences from the last few games to see where we're leaking. We've got challenges coming up over the next two weeks in the form of a tough Memphis team and then Oklahoma City.

"Where'd your Kodashian go?" Rookie asks me. Jay snorts.

It's only then I realize Aliya isn't here.

She had been blowing up my phone, begging me to bring her to this party. I felt bad about bailing the other day, so I caved and said sure, figuring I could use the distraction and she seemed to want to come.

I only have so much power to make dreams come true, so hey, might as well.

On the other side of the room, Brooke's laughing with Nova and Sierra. She always looks good, but tonight, it's as if the universe is out to sing her praises.

Brooke's smile is a million watts. Her blue dress hugs her curves, ending in a school-girl-style skirt high on her toned thighs. Her black hair is swept into pigtails that end along her breasts. Her golden skin gleams in the low light. Dark-red lipstick traces every curve of her mouth, and my dog is parked next to her sparkly red shoes, looking up at her as though she hung the damn moon.

"See something you like?" Jay asks.

My attention snaps back, and I take a drink of my beer. "Just thinking it's a good party."

Brooke's words come back to me.

Take me to Vail. Pretend you're obsessed with me.

She could bring any guy she wanted. No need for pretending.

So, why the hell did she ask me?

Jay follows my gaze, misreading. "I think one of the guys has a thing for her."

"Really." I try not to sound too interested.

"We're already down a man with Atlas out. Don't need to be down two unless there's a solid reason."

If one of the guys on our team hit on our point

guard's sister, it would be a problem. Most of the guys aren't looking for serious relationships, and blowing off steam with another player's family is bad form.

Still..."You're that worried?" I ask.

"She's my baby sister. I always worry. Thought it might stop when she was in college, but nope."

She acts like she's got it all together, confident and secure, but tonight, I saw the smallest crack.

"I'll take care of it." I head for the bar to collect a drink for him and one for me, and for an excuse to see Brooke on the way past.

But when I start back toward Jay, there's no sign of Brooke. Or my dog.

Nova's dancing with Clay, and Sierra's talking with one of the guys from the bench.

"There you are!" Aliya gushes. Her perfume hits me like a brick wall.

"Hey."

Somehow, she's attached to me, her front glued to mine. "Want to get out of here?" she calls over the music.

It's all honeyed sweetness to me, but even I couldn't miss the way she acted with Brooke. It rubbed me the wrong way.

People show you their true selves when they don't want something from you.

"Barely got here and it's Jay's party." The guy is our captain and my friend, and I genuinely want to spend a rare night off with these guys. "You're the one who asked to come," I remind her.

I spot Brooke on the balcony. My dog is still at her feet, but it's her other company that has me taking note.

Rookie.

He's leaning in close, laughing at whatever she said.

Maybe Jay's onto something.

Aliya's hand trails over my shoulder. "How do you like my outfit?"

Rookie's a kid. Barely knows which end of the court to shoot at.

He wouldn't know how to treat her, how to look out for her, how to make her laugh.

"It's nice."

"It'll look even better on your floor."

I frown. "I should stick around for the younger guys for a bit. Set a good example."

"You're a world champion. You should do whatever you want." She shifts closer, her lips getting near my ear. "You can do whatever you want to me."

"Cool." I sip my beer, half my attention on the patio.

When she peels off me, pivoting on her heels and making a beeline for... somewhere else, I should feel bad.

I don't.

Brooke smiles broadly, laughing. When Rookie slides his arm around her waist, it's like a flashing red light.

The last thing we need is Rookie stirring up trouble on the team.

Jay's got his hands full with keeping the team in order, so maybe she needs someone looking out for her.

Someone like me.

I make my way through the crowd, bodies moving before I have to move them. I push through the door and out onto the balcony. The cool air hits me like a slap, but I'm too focused on my destination.

"Hey, Miles!" Rookie greets me with a smile.

"Hey," I say, trying to keep the irritation out of my voice. "You guys having fun?"

"Yeah, we were just talking."

"About?" I prompt, wedging between them.

"What are you—" Brooke starts.

"Nothing to worry about. Sit tight."

I grab Rookie, drag him inside, and shift him—a little harder than necessary—against the wall.

"Whatever you think that is, it's not happening." My voice is pleasant, but the words aren't.

Rookie snorts as though he's not sure whether to laugh or defend himself. "What do you mean?"

I let the smile fade. "I mean, you make a move on Jay's sister, you will not wake up tomorrow morning." I lift my plastic axe. "We have a title to defend this year. It's been a bumpy enough start to the season. You don't fuck with the team, and Brooke is the team."

"Okay! Jeez, I get it." His grin remains, but he reaches up and pats my face. "You need to work on your Kenergy, my dude."

BROOKE

I come up behind Miles and grab a fistful of faux fur, yanking.

The entire vest comes off in my hand.

Cheers go up from people around us, including appreciative noises from the women.

Dammit. I was trying to get Miles's attention, not strip him in the middle of this party.

"What the hell was that?" I demand.

"Huh?" he says.

He's shirtless, and it's distracting. He's tanned from a summer spent outside, his body the kind of perfect that makes me want a closer look at every inch.

To get my hormones under control, I stalk back out to the balcony, and he follows.

"I want to know why you were such a prick to Rookie."

"Fuck, it's freezing out here." He glances at his vest, but I hold it away.

"Explain first. Fur vest second."

He wraps his arms around himself, every muscle in his shoulders, pecs, and arms seeming to flex at once. Miles pulls the door shut behind him and turns back to face me.

"He's a junior guy on the team. There are rules, some of 'em formal and some of 'em you just know."

"And you know better than to tell me I'm one

of those rules." I raise an eyebrow, crossing my arms.

"You know what I mean." He joins me in leaning against the railing.

Jay's house has a view of the mountains. Nature is a sure-fire way to make you feel small.

"It's not only about the Kodiaks," Miles adds. "I don't trust him. He's young and inexperienced."

"I'm a big girl, Miles. Not some helpless damsel in distress."

I take a deep breath of the cool night air and wince, going over on my ankle.

A stream of curses escapes my lips.

"I broke a heel," I explain at Miles's look.

"Sure thing, Princess." His lips twitch.

I bristle. *Oh, no. That's not a nickname I'm letting slide.* "I'm not a princess."

"Look like one to me. Got the shoes. The dress. The hair. The sidekick." He nods to Waffles. "You need backup shoes. Never show up to a game with just one pair."

I open the clip on my bag and wave my cheap slipper flats. "I came prepared, but the Louboutins look better with my costume."

He crooks a finger at me.

"What's that supposed to mean?" I glance

around us, suddenly feeling as if I'm about to be caught on camera for a massive prank.

I typically associate light-headedness with nights in college after too much flavored vodka. Or the time I played a high school basketball tournament and got so competitive and focused on watching the other teams' games in between ours that I forgot to eat for an entire day.

But as Miles sinks to one knee at my feet, the blood is rushing to places that are not my head.

His fingers brush my skin as he takes my ankle in his hand. A not-unpleasant shiver runs up my spine.

What the fuck.

He slides off my heel, setting it on the deck where Waffles is huffing excitedly.

Music drifts from the other side of the glass doors. Inside, familiar and unfamiliar people dressed as pop stars and ghouls and superheroes laugh and drink and dance.

Out here, we're alone.

Miles takes a slipper from my grip.

I'm so surprised I don't think to resist when he slides it onto my foot.

"There."

He switches to the other side. Heat spreads

through my body. Sparks light me up. The feel of him touching me is strangely intimate.

Suddenly, I'm wondering what would happen if his hands traveled up my calf to my thigh and...

"Done." Miles's gaze lingers on my legs. "Not worth twisting an ankle."

"Beauty is pain," I say lightly.

"You look good enough without them."

Miles straightens to his full height, the moon generously highlighting the planes of his cut torso and shoulders. The words wrap around me the way he was wrapping his arms around himself a moment ago.

I'm more than a little drunk and tempted to drop his vest over the edge of the balcony for the good of humankind.

"Why do you want a date?" he asks.

I pull my brain out of the alternate universe in which I'm respectfully licking his chest.

"There's a contract I want to win with this alum who'll be there." I don't want to explain the details or how my competition is bringing my ex. "The entire weekend is a big social test, and it helps to have backup."

Miles raises an eyebrow. "Backup with an

axe?" He hooks the shoes on the plastic blade of the axe and lets both dangle from his grip.

"No." I laugh. *Is he going to make me say it?* "Someone good looking, popular, charming."

Miles studies me for a moment, his expression unreadable. "Brooke."

"What?" I'm instantly suspicious.

He steps closer to me, his hand brushing a strand of hair away from my face. "You don't need to prove anything to anyone."

I feel myself warm, both from his words and the heat radiating off his body. "That's not what I'm doing—"

His mouth firms into a line. "I'm in."

My brows shoot up, a laugh in my throat. "You're uninvited."

"I'm reinviting myself."

My mouth falls open. Miles always knows how to surprise me. "It's the weekend after next. Friday night to Sunday morning."

"No game until Monday." He grins. "It's a date."

6

BROOKE

To: belliso3@alumni.cc.edu
From: kappapastpresident@alumni.cc.edu
Subject: URGENT – RSVP AND REQUEST!

Dear Brooke,

It's ten days until the reunion, and you haven't told us the name of your plus-one! If it was anyone else, I'd tell them the cutoff was two weeks ago. But we're sisters, so I'll let it slide.

Speaking of, can you sort the seating chart for dinner? I'm attaching it, and I haven't got a spare moment. Whatever you do, you MUST put us at the same table. We have so much to catch up on.

Love,

Caroline

P.S. There's no shame in not bringing a date. It's terribly modern.

~

"*H*ow's living the glamorous life as a big-city doctor?" I ask as I sweep in the front door of my building with a smile for the doorman.

"Double shifts with a ham on rye. I'm living the dream." Ruby holds up her wrapped sandwich over FaceTime.

I laugh.

My apartment building is in a great location. I can walk to lots of places. I wave to the concierge and pick up my mail before heading upstairs, doing a silent fist pump when I see a package that must be the vibe I ordered. "I'm making a pitch for Elise and thought you might have some advice since you overlapped."

I've been up working on it all night, pacing my apartment.

"Her room was next to mine the first year I was a sister," Ruby confirms. "She was cooler than most of the girls—driven, but everyone in that house was."

"What does she like?"

"She appreciates ambition. I remember she headed up three different committees at once. I know we all like to say, 'I don't know how she does it,' but truly... I don't know how she does it."

I take the stairs, for the cardio and because the cell reception has a tendency to cut out.

"I've got to make this work, Rubes," I vow.

I need the money.

I didn't work in high school because I played basketball and we traveled for Jay's tournaments. I volunteered for several non-profits but I'm guessing they don't pay the kind of money I need to maintain my lifestyle.

Plus, a part of me would love to prove that I'm fine without my mom's support doing exactly what I'm doing.

Living a fabulous life and posting about it.

"You'll crush it. How will it be to see Kevin again?"

The back of my neck feels damp under my

hair. "It's in the past. I've put everything about him behind me."

Upstairs, I let myself into my apartment. My floor-to-ceiling windows on two sides have views of the mountains.

Every day I wake up and throw the curtains open, I feel like I can do anything, be anyone.

"You don't have to pretend with me," Ruby says.

"I'm not." I step out of my shoes, leaving them haphazardly next to half a dozen other pairs. "Did his actions back then mess with me? Sure. But in the end, he did me a favor."

When I drop the mail on the quartz counter, a bank statement slides out from the bottom.

"I can't wait to see you in person. Is Tim coming?" I ask.

"No, he's busy. It's girl time."

"Please tell me your husband is pulling his weight while you do all these shifts."

"He's busy at work too."

As she talks, I tear into the envelope.

I have almost no money left, but I'm too embarrassed to volunteer that to Ruby, who put herself through medical school.

"I'm actually bringing someone. I thought it would help present a solid front to Elise."

"And you didn't lead with this?! Which boy will be desperately clinging to your arm?"

I tuck the bank statement under the other mail and round the counter to the living room, sinking into my plush couch. "Miles. He's my brother's teammate."

"Standby while I look this guy up." She frowns and types away, her brows rising. "Little Sis, you've been holding out on me."

I laugh. "I'm not interested in a boyfriend. It's one weekend only."

"You'll be sharing a room. Making eyes at each other. Flirting and laughing and cuddling."

Now I'm imagining doing those things with him.

"What about Hannah? Is she going?" Ruby's question brings me back.

"I haven't heard from her lately." One of the handful of sisters I keep up with regularly since graduation was a year ahead of me and one behind Ruby. She was partly responsible for me pledging, being the smiling face who helped recruit me, and one of the few sisters I knew I could take any of my school problems to.

"Being partner track at her firm in New York probably doesn't leave much time for a social life."

"True, but Caroline will love that. Hannah was always part of her carefully curated collection of friends."

Ruby rolls her eyes. "You ever regret pledging?"

"No, because I met you."

Ruby knows firsthand the daily challenges of being Black in a white sorority—all the girls who'd say loudly that they were color blind but in the next breath, they were fascinated by your hair or impressed by your family's seamless integration into the state's political fabric.

We each had our own reasons not to pledge a historically Black sorority. For me, I did it for my mom.

She wanted me in this sorority because it was full of high achievers in business, law, and medicine, and it presented the right image.

Like my mom, it wasn't as if the sorority had explicit expectations. More like there were unspoken ideals, and the fact that Jay and I came from a family where success and education was important meant we should be successful too.

Didn't matter that Jay wanted to play

basketball. Once he got an athletic scholarship, then was drafted into the NBA, his image proved to poll surprisingly well for my mom.

Me on the other hand...

One night of mayhem and a near scandal in college ruined that.

"You've always had my back, Ruby. With what happened junior year..." I shake my head. "I wouldn't have made it through without you."

She sighs. "It gets pretty lonely even in a house full of girls. We all need allies. If Miles is going to be that for you, then I'm glad you're bringing him."

7

MILES

*P*eople think my life is all glamorous, but it's not.

Sure, I make millions, have an agent who fields requests for my time, and my dog has a fan page with more followers than there were people in the small town I grew up in.

Otherwise, I have the same issues as anyone else.

Like when I go to sign in at the front desk of the single-story building, glancing around the unmanned station for a pen.

Nothing.

I skip out on the sign-in sheet and make my way down the hall.

A light flickers overhead, but when I glance up, it comes back on.

As I continue on my path, a man rounds the corner in front of me. His eyes are narrowed, but it's hard to focus on them when he's wearing a dressing gown hanging open and nothing underneath.

"You," he accuses.

I place a hand on my chest. "Me?"

"Yes, you. You turned off my music."

"So I did. Let me make it up to you, Mr. P."

I tilt my head and walk side by side with him down to the lounge. We put on the record player, and I get him settled with one of the staff before I continue on my way.

In the two years I've been coming here, the residents have come and gone, but Mr. P is a fixture.

I knock on Grams's door, but there's no answer. I let myself in, edging the door open a crack. Inside, she's sitting in her chair, her eyes closed as if she's asleep. I approach her slowly, not wanting to startle her.

"Grams?" I say, kneeling beside her.

She opens her eyes and smiles, taking my hand. "Hello, dear. It's good to see you. How's my boy?"

"He still tracks dirt on the sofa."

"I meant you, not Waffles."

"So did I."

She laughs, her eyes crinkling.

It's good to see her like this, happy and sharp. There are days her expression is bright and lively and others she's tired. I've looked enough that I can tell instantly what kind of day it is, almost before she starts to speak.

"I brought you flowers." I hold up a bouquet of daisies and sunflowers. "And cookies. I haven't figured out how to smuggle Waffles in yet but we're working on it."

"Ahh. Thank you, honey. I watched your game the other night."

"What'd you think?"

"You played wonderfully."

"You have to say that."

"Untrue. If you played terribly, I'd let you know."

I grin. "You still getting to your workout classes?" They have in-chair mobility three days a week.

"I'd like to get out for the dance. It should be next weekend," she says, "but I haven't heard."

"I'll check with the staff, see if there's anything planned."

"I used to love dancing with your grandfather."

I feel a pang at the mention of my grandfather, who passed away when I was young. I know how much he meant to my grandma, and I'm glad she has those memories to hold on to.

"What are you doing when you have a day off?" she prompts.

"I'm going to a sorority reunion. With a friend."

Her eyes brighten. "A lady friend?"

"Maybe." I chuckle, knowing she's trying to play matchmaker.

After I headed home from the party, Brooke's broken shoes somehow tucked under my arm, I found myself scrolling through her socials.

Nearly a quarter of a million followers. Princess is building a little empire of her own.

I'm not one of them, because if I looked at her posts on a regular basis, I'd probably have to leave a heart on them.

And if I did that, then I wouldn't be able to help leaving a comment.

If I left a comment, I'd have to watch my mouth.

Otherwise, her brother would crawl so far up my ass that he'd feel firsthand the way my heart speeds up when she's around and read into it.

"You deserve someone," Grams says softly.

"I don't need someone."

"That's not the same thing."

My attention drifts to the family photos along one wall.

"Not every relationship is like your and grandpa's," I say.

"Not every relationship is like your parents' either," she fills in.

I shake my head because as much as I try to indulge her, she's more romantic than I am.

I glance at the coffee table, cracking my knuckles. "We better get down to business. You rethink the offer on Park Place?"

"Only if you're getting out of railroads."

I sink into the chair opposite her across the Monopoly board, and we get down to it.

The box of cookies gets busted open, and even though she insists I partake, I only have one, leaving the rest for her.

Money goes back and forth. Winning isn't the point. The point is to keep the game going.

She starts to yawn, which means it's time for

her nap. I stick my pile of cash in one corner and point at it.

"Don't go collecting interest on this without me," I warn.

She smiles and wraps her arms around my waist, as high as she can reach.

"Miles, you have a kind heart," she says, squeezing me. "Don't be afraid to let someone in."

"I love you, Grams." I bend to drop a kiss on her gray hair.

On my way out, I spot one of the staff, a young woman who waves me off distractedly until recognition lights up her face. "Hey, Miles."

"Hey, Trina. My grams was asking about an event, this dance thing?"

"We had to cancel it. Our social coordinator quit last week."

That's probably why the music was out in the lounge too.

"The light is flickering in the hallway."

She nods absently. "Got it."

"Let me fix it while I'm here."

"No. You don't need to."

I lift a brow and head for the custodian's closet.

"It's an old building," Trina calls after me. "Sometimes things just don't work right."

"Bad news, gentlemen—Atlas is out indefinitely," Coach informs us grimly.

The gym falls silent.

In the corner, one of the cleaners whistles to a song on his headphones as he mops.

"What happened to day-to-day?" Jay demands.

"New set of scans came back. There's a bone fracture we didn't see."

Clay rubs a hand over his face. Jay paces as if he can make sense of it.

There's no making sense. There's just you and the basketball gods, and today they decided we aren't going to have a full roster.

"Miles." Coach calls me over once the group starts running drills. "We need you to step up with Atlas out."

"You got it. I've been working on my shot all summer."

"Shooting from the outside's not enough. You've got to be physical. Getting into the paint. Driving and kicking it out to your teammates. High-level footwork. Finishing at the rim."

I frown. "None of that's how I've built my game."

Coach sighs. "This team's going to have to change things up if we want to win."

I stare after him as he rejoins the assistants.

What the hell does that mean?

His words stick with me as we get back to practice. Passing, guarding, free throws, three-pointers—I work through the drills I know in my body even more than my head. Been doing them for years, even before I turned pro.

I always loved to play basketball, loved being around other guys who feel the same. As a kid going through tough times, each day my fingers touched the ball, that I got paid to run around a court, it was a joy.

In high school, I had the most points of any shooting guard in the state. My college team got to Final Four once, division champs twice.

Sure, I'm not intense to the point of self-destruction like Clay or strategic like Jay. My magic on the court is being a sharpshooter, but in the locker room, I'm a glue guy.

I made some mistakes as a rookie, did things I'm not proud of. I finished out college ball and got my degree before getting drafted to Dallas. Then the chance came to move here a few years ago, be back playing with Jay, and it felt right.

Thing is, I'm worth the most I'll ever be right now. I'm not twenty-one like Rookie, not an MVP like Clay. I have to make my money now and be smart about how I manage it.

Especially with Grams depending on me.

Seeing the gaps at her home was a reminder that I need to keep my eye on her and support her to the best of my ability.

I work on my jump shot for an hour until it's just me and a couple of other guys. I hit a shot off the iron, and it bounces wild.

My phone vibrates from my gym bag, and I go over to check it.

Brooke: We need to talk about your wardrobe for next weekend. What clothes do you have?

I glance down as I reach the locker room.

Miles: Right now, sweaty ones.

I take a pic and send it.
Dots appear, then stop.

Brooke: Gross.

Miles: Let me guess, Princess, you don't sweat. You glisten?

Brooke: Listen, you have to look good, or this whole game is over before it's started.

I'm a little offended she thinks I would bring her image down. I'm used to being part of the team, repping the Kodiaks and my teammates. If you ask Chloe, head of PR, each of us is our own brand, and mine's doing fine. Better than fine.

Miles: You want to come over to my place and go through my closet?

It's a joke, and a challenge. Me calling her on being a little overenthusiastic about this entire sorority weekend ploy.

I glance up as Clay and one of our young guys cross the room, towels slung over their shoulders.

The shower is beckoning.

Brooke: Deal. See you tomorrow.

My brows lift.

I'm edgy from the news of Atlas being out and what Coach said about my game. Spending an afternoon flipping through my closet with Brooke feels like the last thing I need to do.

Except the prospect of doing exactly that has me wondering what it'd be like.

On impulse, I go on her social. Her video story is of her walking from a car to the party in her sparkly shoes. The camera flashes glimpses of long, golden legs as she strides up the driveway. She's laughing, talking about how she's going to find Toto and get the hell out of Kansas.

My lips curve without permission, my thumb hovering over the Follow button.

"You forget where the showers are?" Rookie claps a hand on my shoulder, and I jump, dropping the phone into my locker.

When I grab for the phone, I realize I clicked Follow.

No take-backs.

It's fine. Nothing weird about following her.

If we're spending the entire weekend together next week, it only makes sense.

8

BROOKE

*M*y knock is casual. Three raps.

Miles's door is painted cream like all the others in this high-end condo building, but standing in front of it feels different.

There's nothing unusual about me showing up at his place on the weekend. His place, where he eats and sleeps and probably bangs anything that moves.

Except I've never been here before. Miles has been on the team as long as my brother, and since I graduated college, across the dozen Kodiaks parties and events I've been to, I never wound up here.

Come to think of it, I'm not sure he's ever hosted one. For a guy who's so outgoing and popular, it's surprising.

I'm dressed in heeled boots and a short skirt over black tights. If I spent extra time getting ready, it was only to prove to him or the world that what you wear matters.

I'm not my mother—I don't have constituents imposing all their opinions on me—but it's still important to present yourself to the world intentionally. I'm here to make sure he has appropriate clothing for the reunion. No matter how hot he is, there's no point bringing him if he can't walk the walk.

Everything is about appearances.

"Miles, it's me," I call, my voice echoing down the hallway.

Barking sounds through the door. *Waffles.*

There's a moment of silence before the door opens. The Frenchie barrels toward me, but it's Miles, shirtless and still damp from a shower, that hijacks my attention.

His massive frame fills the doorway, blocking out the light at his back.

Gray sweatpants cling to muscled legs and hips. His ridiculously cut pecs and abs are on full display. Sleepy blue eyes are fringed with dark lashes.

He smells clean and fresh and addictive. His

jaw is razor-sharp and smooth shaven, and I ignore the itch to stretch up a hand and run a finger along it.

I've been around athletes my entire life. Through my brother's friends in school, I've seen the gross things they pull, the ways they smell, the jokes they tell. I decided years ago that I'm immune to whatever charms they think they have.

But as I soak in all six-four of Miles, I'm weak.

"Hey." His voice is low and easy, reminding me why he's the coolest fucker in the entire Western Conference.

I force myself to tear my gaze away from his body and look him in the eyes. "Glad you didn't dress up."

He shrugs a muscled shoulder with an easy grace. "Figured you were dressing me up, so it didn't matter what I started in."

"Whatever you say, debate team captain." I walk past him, trying to ignore the way his scent lingers in the air.

"Do I sense sarcasm?" He lets the door swing shut after me. "I was very book smart in college."

"Long as they're picture books. With boobs."

"I love all books equally. Even the ones with boobs."

His apartment is modern and minimalistic, and there are no dirty dishes or clothes lying around. It's as though he actually takes care of himself.

I slip off my boots and follow him into the kitchen. The place is immaculate, everything in its place and not a speck of dust in sight. I always imagined him living in an expensive bachelor pad with beer cans and pizza boxes strewn about. But this place looks as if it belongs in a magazine.

Probably his housekeeper.

Miles gestures to the kitchen. "Almond milk latte?"

"Sure." I'm surprised he remembers as I follow him to the counter. Waffles whines at my feet, and I bend to pick him up. "You're heavier than you look."

Miles shoots me a perplexed look. "He doesn't like it when I pick him up."

"You clearly don't have the right touch."

"Never had any complaints."

His easy response strokes along my skin like a promise.

He's used to women falling at his feet. Even if I'm a little wobbly on mine, I'd die before I let on.

"Let's get something straight before we go any

further," I start. "We might be committing to the act next weekend, but nothing is real."

Miles opens his cupboard and retrieves a bag of espresso beans as if he hasn't heard me.

"Got it?" I call over the whirring of the grinder as he gets to work.

No idea how he doesn't burn himself, being half naked while he steams milk, but he manages.

More than manages.

I never thought a guy making coffee was hot before, but this is some serious competence porn.

He pours the coffee, and I set the dog back down. The heat emanating from his body is too much to ignore, and I find myself leaning closer.

"It smells good," I say.

He glances down at me. "So do you."

My throat dries.

Didn't have "add 'hot guy making coffee' to my fantasy list" on my bingo card for today.

I'm here because I need a date who will make it easier for me to land this contract so I can pay my bills. It's not a chill day off for me like it is for him.

"I mean it." My voice is higher than it was a moment ago. "Next weekend, there will be a lot of acting involved, but no matter how method things get, it's not real."

"Did you get a new phone yet?"

I shake my head and set mine on the counter.

He traces a finger along the cracked screen. "You're not the type to make do, Princess."

I shrug a shoulder. "I hear suffering builds character. That reminds me..."

I reach into my purse and pull out five one-hundred-dollar bills. "Waffles's management's share from the costume contest."

I hold them toward him, though what I want to do is shove them back in my pocket.

"Keep it. He told me he had a good time."

I arch a brow, gratitude rushing up as I put the bills back in my bag.

The money is nothing to him. This week, it means a lot to me.

Miles slides over the drink and waits for me to take a sip. "Tell me that's not the best thing you've had in your mouth."

I sip my coffee, the complex flavors dancing on my tongue.

"It's good," I admit.

"Fuck yeah, it is." His grin is pure male satisfaction, as if I just conceded that he rocked my world.

I take another sip. God, the contrast between

the bitterness of the coffee and the sweetness from the milk makes my taste buds do a happy dance.

Focus.

"We need to make sure you look like the perfect Kappa boyfriend," I say, steepling my fingers. "That means new clothes."

"I have clothes."

He heads down the hall, motioning with a hand for me to follow as Waffles trots after him.

Following isn't a hardship.

The way those sweatpants cling to Miles's hips has my fingers tightening on my mug.

His room is as clean and tidy as the rest of his apartment. The bed is neatly made. I can't help but glance around, taking in the details of his personal space. There's a guitar propped up against the wall and a set of weights in the corner. On the bedside table sits a photo of him and the guys from the team after winning the championship.

"After you." He holds open the door of the walk-in closet, and I go in first.

I take in the side that's been converted entirely into basketball shoe storage. "Of course you have this many shoes."

Miles joins me in the closet, leaning an elbow on my shoulder. "Gotta have options on the court."

"This is a weird question, but did you see my shoes from the other night?"

"Not sure. You left them on the balcony. Weren't they broken?" He says it with the casualness of someone who could replace them fifty times over on a single day's salary.

"Right."

They were also some of my favorites, but I push the grief aside.

I ask about formal wear, and he points to some jackets at one end.

"That's all the formal wear you have?"

"Don't make my money in a tux, Princess."

I run my hand over a navy suit, feeling the rough material. "These are too small."

He strips down to his shorts, and I catch my lip between my teeth as I turn away. He pulls on the pants, and I swivel back to take him in.

"Huh. You're right," he says, tugging for a millimeter of spare fabric in his pants. "Coach figured I could put on ten pounds of muscle this summer."

"And did you?"

"Nah, I put on twenty."

It's fake, I remind myself.

But I can ogle my fake boyfriend a little, right? Just to get into the proper headspace.

"Well, we need to find you something that fits," I say, glancing up at him. "Time to go shopping."

We take Miles's Range Rover.

On the way, I admit I haven't eaten, and he insists on stopping at a Mexican fast-food place. He orders six tortillas, and I get two and a Diet Coke.

"So, you and Jay, you're three years apart."

"Two and a half," I correct. "He was a winter baby. I was summer."

"Your family's a pretty big deal."

"My mom got into politics when I was young. Never looked back."

"A lot of cameras."

"Less than being in the NBA," I quip.

"Yeah, but at least we know when we're on camera."

I turn that over. "Society holds women to impossible standards. Jay can do whatever he wants, as long as he's employed and stays on the right side of the law, and he's golden. For me, I can't wear a skirt too short or swear or express opinions different from my mom's. People have an opinion on how much I work and who my friends are."

"Sounds rough."

I unwrap my lunch, aware of his gaze resting on me. I don't want to harp on it and I'm grateful for what I have. "You know my family, but I don't know much about yours," I say as I bite into my food.

"Not much to know. I was an only child. My parents split up when I was young. My grandma is my biggest fan, always telling me how proud she is, and she's been doing it since high school."

His eyes light up when he mentions her. It's sweet, and it makes me feel warm and soft inside.

"You guys are close."

"She raised me herself. Took me in after... well, after a lot of shit went down."

He doesn't talk much about his life before basketball. He's always seemed like the carefree guy who makes it look easy. I never stopped to think he might have as many problems as anyone else behind the quick grin and the flirting.

"So, why don't you have a real boyfriend to dress up and bring to this thing?"

I arch a brow. "I've never met a guy I liked enough to keep."

"I'm down for this game you're playing, but you're doing a helluva dance for people you don't really like."

"I never said I didn't like them. I don't trust them."

"What's the difference? You have to trust the people you like."

Miles reaches across the table and grabs my Diet Coke. He takes a sip, face contorting. "That is disgusting."

I grab it back from him, sipping with narrowed eyes until my soda's gone entirely.

After lunch, we head to a boutique to find Miles some new clothes. The assistant comes over to help. She's making eyes at Miles, and I tell her we have things under control.

I load him up with clothes, our hands brushing. "Try these on."

"Say please." He's goading me. I think this man gets off on pushing my buttons.

I roll my eyes. "Do it."

The employee eyes me from across the room with admiration and envy as Miles disappears into the changing room.

I've never spent this much time with him, certainly not just the two of us.

He's maddening, but our banter is slightly addictive.

I pace outside the changing room, waiting for him to come out. My mind is racing with thoughts of him in those clothes, wondering how they'll fit.

"What are *you* wearing?" he asks me through the door.

"I have a few outfits picked out."

"What about that dress from the party the other night? With the stockings."

"It was a Halloween costume," I say.

"So... no Dorothy role-playing."

I snort. "Storybook characters do it for you?"

"You say that like it's a red flag."

"Isn't it?"

"Beige at most. Tell me you don't have any kinks."

"None you need to know about to take me to the sorority event."

"More I know about you, the more authentic it will be."

"The point isn't to be real. It's to be convincing."

"Yeah, and for the next week, we're on the

same team. So, tell me about this sorority thing," he says. His voice comes from lower than I expect, as if he's bent over to pull on pants. "Is it all braiding each other's hair and singing songs?"

"No." I try to sound indignant, but there is some of that too. "The afternoon we arrive, there are games, followed by dinner. After is sisters-only business, so you have some free time. Your job is to be the perfect date throughout. An attractive accessory."

"So, a trophy."

"Exactly. The girls should want to be with you. The guys should want to be you."

I don't tell him he probably has a lock on that already just by being himself.

"Right. Any conversation topics to avoid?"

"All of them. In fact, don't speak. If they speak to you, better if you answer in monosyllables."

"You could take a mannequin from the store instead. Maybe he'd come with the clothes."

Miles comes out of the changing room, and I'm not prepared for the sight.

The camel quarter-zip cashmere sweater is a few shades lighter than his hair. The gray chinos cling to his hips.

"How do I look?" A dimple appears, and God, it's unfair for one person to be so lethally attractive.

He's so fucking hot I'm a breath from asking the store to turn on the air conditioning even though it's the end of October.

The sweater and chinos make him preppy, but there's a rough edge to him. The dark hair and cut jaw and arrogant eyes would set him apart from a million former frat boys. He's as at home in these clothes as he was in sweatpants answering his door.

"You look okay," I concede.

"Just okay?" He cocks his head.

"I'm not feeding your ego."

"Do it, Princess. I'm fucking starved for validation." His teasing makes my teeth want to bite my lip.

The sales associate comes in and gasps. "You look... wow."

He turns that grin on her. I can practically see her ovaries melt.

"You need these to fall like this..." I step between them and bend down to adjust the hem of his pants.

"So, who's the competition?" Miles asks me.

"Hmmm?"

I tip my face up and realize I'm on my knees in front of him.

His lashes are lowered as he peers down at me, lips parted and head cocked.

It's sexy as hell.

"For this deal you're trying to land."

"Right." I shake off the position we're in. "Caroline. She was sorority president my junior and senior year."

"Why would your alum pick her over you?"

"Because Caroline is perfect."

The grid on her social is full of summer parties in the Hamptons, days by the pool, premieres in LA, nightclub openings in New York. She has more followers than me.

"Good thing you have a secret weapon."

"What's that?" I rise, my shirt brushing his sweater.

His slow grin is pure confidence. "Me."

MILES

*A*ll afternoon, Brooke and I have been playing dress-up.

I'm six-four, so finding clothes is no slam dunk, yet she scans the racks with her critical eye, pulling garments that magically fit me.

As for her, she looks way too distracting, her outfit skimming her curves, her hair pulled back and plum lipstick on.

I'm pretty sure bossing me around turns her on.

She was the one who wanted to get clear on the boundaries, but every time she inspects me with those dark eyes, I wonder how wide they'd get if I backed her into the wall and slipped a hand up her skirt.

I'm supposed to be looking out for her, not

imagining the things we could do in this dressing room before the sales associate busted us.

"I have to be back for shootaround," I say through the door after she approves the last outfit I emerged in.

"Just one more?"

I pull on another shirt and button it.

I've got a game in a few hours, which is what I should be focused on with the team pressure of Atlas being out—that or my grandma's well-being.

Not Brooke's laugh, her eyes.

Not why she doesn't have an actual date to take to this event.

She always displays this utter confidence, so hearing her express nerves over her competition is surprising.

It doesn't turn me off to see this side of her. If anything, her letting me in has the opposite effect.

She's beautiful, with walls she keeps high on purpose. I'm allowed to wonder what it would be like to peel away everything and see what's left.

"Did you get stuck in there?" she calls, sounding impatient.

I'm the most relaxed guy in every locker room, but the last half an hour she's locked her feelings down and gone back to tough Brooke.

Her annoyance has me reaching for the door.

Fuck the buttons.

I step out of the changing room. "You think you can do it faster?"

She's right outside, turning to face me when I emerge.

Her eyes widen as she takes me in, the shirt hanging open. There's a flash of awareness.

I like getting under her skin. I could live there a minute.

We're inches apart when her fingers go to my shirt, brushing mine out of the way.

"You have big hands," she murmurs. Her lips are parted, her lashes half lowered as she focuses on her work.

"Thanks. I do some of my best work with them." I grin.

Her manicure is bright blue, the color of the ocean in the Caribbean.

"How is the season going?" she asks as she works her way down from the top button.

She grazes my abs. I want to grab her hand and slide it lower.

I don't often share my personal struggles, but her point-blank question makes me want to answer, and the back of this boutique feels private.

"I worked this summer on my shooting, and I got better. Except I don't know if better is good enough with us being short-handed."

She finishes with the buttons and adjusts the cuffs. Her wrists are small. I could circle them with my thumb and pinkie.

"There must be something you can do. Maybe you're holding yourself back." She tilts her face up, showing me those gorgeous dark eyes.

The comment catches me off guard.

"It's not high school, Princess. We can't play scrappy and cover each other's spots. This is a professional league, and every guy has to slot in."

"Even if I agreed with you on that, there's more you could try. Dig in. Get tough. Take things personally."

Brooke stands on her toes, reaching up to adjust my collar.

"Oh, like you do?" I ask.

She wobbles, and I catch her waist with one hand to steady her. She's warm through her shirt, her stomach soft under my thumb.

I don't wear a lot of collared shirts, but I might need to start.

"Last year," she gives me side-eye, "you had a goal to fight for. You were underdogs. But now, you have nothing to prove. The entire team can sit around in a massive circle jerk and reminisce about your glory days."

"That's not true," I say.

"Isn't it?" Her chin lifts. "You play the same game, date the same girls. Maybe you need more to motivate you."

My smile slips.

I take three steps forward, and she nearly trips trying to keep up. Her back flattens against the wall, and I put a hand on either side of her head.

"You want to dish it out, you better be able to take it," I say.

Her big, dark eyes blink up at me. "What does that mean?"

She's not telling me the whole truth. It started earlier with her phone, the cracked screen she ignored when I know for a fact she likes everything perfect.

"There's a reason you want this contract so much that you're willing to go to these lengths to get it."

She dismisses the question. "I'm competitive."

"Yeah, that's not it."

She looks away, and I capture her chin in my thumb and forefinger.

Every second she doesn't answer and I don't release her, the tension between us escalates.

Her lashes lower, her lips pressing together. "My mom cut me off." Her grimace is disgusted, but under that, there's shame. Hurt.

"Cut you off," I echo, releasing her chin. "How much of your life was she paying for?"

Brooke inspects her nails. "A lot, apparently. That's why I need to land this gig with Elise. And it's down to me and Caroline, and I don't only want it..."

"You need it," I finish as the pieces click together. "So why don't you ask Jay?"

"Because he could snap his fingers and put me on an allowance, which would make him think he has more of a say in how I live my life than he already does. I'm not going from one person paying my rent to someone else doing it."

I know how much pressure there is in this world to meet expectations. Even in basketball, guys constantly have new houses, new cars, new businesses. I'm lucky as hell to be in the position where I can afford things I couldn't dream of as a kid, but I'm not immune to it.

Between her mom's political career and Jay's basketball career, Brooke grew up with an audience. As much as she resents having to appear flawless, she wants to feel put together, and she wants to do it on her own.

I get it.

Her big, dark eyes find mine. "Don't tell Jay."

The firmness of her request has me blinking. "About getting cut off or that I'm going as your date?"

"Either."

Fuck. I don't like where this is going.

"He's going to find out." The resistance rising up has me shaking my head. "There'll be pics from the event."

"You said yourself the team is in flux. Just wait it out. Tell him in a few weeks." Her expression turns pleading. "I don't want him thinking less of me."

I don't like keeping secrets from my friend and teammate. Honesty is a big deal to me, especially with guys I line up shoulder to shoulder with to face the world.

But...

I want to be here for Brooke. For all the tough acts she puts on, she's vulnerable.

I wrestle with it until the alarm on my phone

goes off, reminding me I have a few minutes to get my ass in gear.

"On one condition," I say. "If you need anything, you come to me."

"No." The word is out of her lips before I finish.

"I mean it. Promise me." I stare down at her with my most serious expression.

Her full mouth purses. "Fine."

"I lied. There are two conditions."

She throws up her hands to protest but I grab her wrists. Her pulse kicks under my thumbs, warm and vital.

"You want to dress me up, I get to play dress up with you too, Princess."

BROOKE

You are cordially invited to a Fundraiser

**Hosted by Women's Leadership Society
of Colorado**

**November 12, 12:00PM
Denver Library
Lunch will be served**

~

With my mom going on the campaign trail next year, she's in what Jay and I like to call her warm-up phase.

I can hear her voice saying, "*It's never too early to form a good impression.*"

I hear it almost as clearly as her saying that bad impressions last longer than good ones.

"I thought you were going to straighten your hair?" Mom adjusts the sleeves on her navy crepe suit. She has a way of fussing while looking perfectly relaxed. Just in case anyone's taking pictures.

I clasp my hands lightly behind my back. I know the tricks too. "I thought this looked better."

Her gaze runs down my body. "Is that new?"

"Mhmm."

The navy Michael Kors polo dress skims my curves and stops just past the knee. It's not the most revealing thing in my closet, but the moment my eye lingered a beat on the garment, Miles was pointing for the sales associate to wrap it up, along with two other dresses.

I didn't need him to buy me clothes, but he made me promise in exchange for keeping my secret from Jay. Maybe a small part of me wanted to enjoy it, since it's probably the last time I'll be shopping for a while.

Mom's perfectly threaded brows draw together. "Honey. I know you think my ending our financial arrangement is unfounded, but I promise it will only help you build character."

I paste on a smile, spared having to respond to her comment when my brother arrives wearing a sweater and chinos.

His presence relieves her, too. "Jayden, thank you for coming. I know how busy you are."

Jay's gaze connects with mine and we exchange a sibling look. *Mom being mom.*

"Good game the other night," she continues without noticing. "You sit at table four. Brooke, you're at six. I have prospective donors you should speak with. I don't need to tell you to be on your best behavior."

We knew coming here meant Mom would pimp us out. Families of politicians are some of the hardest working unpaid interns.

But I do my duty, sit next to the wife of a finance guy during a lecture about education.

"Did you love being in a sorority? Our Adele is making decisions for college next year," she says, declining her dessert with an easy smile at the waiter.

"Absolutely. It was a big commitment, but I made lifelong friendships."

That part was true. It brought me to Ruby,

Hannah, and a few other women I keep in touch with because I genuinely enjoy them, not because we or our parents are in the same circles.

My brother meets me at the bar. "God, I figured once we were adults we wouldn't get roped into the circus."

"Are you a clown or one of those seals with a ball on its nose?" I ask.

"I think I'm the trapeze artist, trying to remember which way is up while he flips in every direction." His grin fades. "Everything okay with you and Mom?"

"Of course. Why?"

A shrug. "Just a vibe."

I don't want to tell him what's happening because, as much as the reason for Mom cutting me off is bullshit, I can see my brother swooping in and fixing things.

They each have their own world that revolves around them. The political world exists for my mom. Jay pretends to get it, but he doesn't really because he lives in his own world too. The basketball world, where he's the star and he's worshipped.

Yesterday, I read an editorial by a college grad who had been expecting a huge trust fund.

Because of some family issues, it never came through. It completely derailed her life.

That's not happening to me. I refuse to be the butt of a joke.

A roaming photographer's presence reminds me to document. *Pics or it didn't happen.*

"Bring it in, fam." I motion Jay closer, and he gets the assignment, leaning in and lifting the phone from my fingers to snap the selfie while we display matching smiles.

We take the picture, and I post it along with one I took of my mom speaking with a little caption.

"So, Garrett helped you out."

Jay's comment makes me jump. "Miles? How did you..."

"I'm surprised he let you use Waffles for your costume at the party."

"Oh." Relief washes over me. "It was too perfect to pass up."

My brother frowns. "He's protective of that little dude. Belonged to his grandma or something." Someone catches Jay's eye and he heads out across the room, leaving me to think alone.

Spending time with Miles was even more fun than I expected.

Sure, he's gorgeous in everything from sweatpants to sorority-reunion best. I've caught myself remembering half a dozen times how his hard abs felt under my fingers, wondering if his mouth would be as cocky and confident on mine.

"If you need anything, you come to me."

I vowed after Kevin that I'd never trust another guy to have my back.

Still, how Miles acted makes me wonder if maybe there are trustworthy guys in the world.

It's probably bullshit. Like unicorns and the tooth fairy and nonfat ice cream that actually tastes good.

Mom makes a reappearance. "Did you see Kevin's parents over there?"

I force myself to straighten. "We don't talk."

It's one thing to schmooze for the family business, but I draw the line at voluntarily engaging with the people who spawned my ex.

"Well, you're about to start. Kevin's with them."

My head snaps around to find familiar dark eyes, perfectly cut and styled dirty-blond hair.

The sight of him hits me like a dark, twisted cocktail with the aftertaste of a long, bad night.

I turn away, hoping he gets the message. He was always more subtle than me.

"Kevin was the best thing that could have happened to you," she sighs. "I wish you'd seen it sooner."

A headache twinges at my temple.

Mom's swept off to glad-hand more donors, and I make the rounds until I lose sight of Kevin. I've managed to avoid him completely when I duck into the bathroom for a moment to breathe.

The woman in the mirror looks composed. I touch up my makeup anyway.

My ex fit with my mother's plans. I'd thought he fit with mine. Every sorority sister envied us.

He ripped it all away.

Seeing his face for the first time in so long, I'm not sure my heart healed so much as formed scar tissue.

I'm going to charm Elise and score a brand ambassadorship right out from under Caroline, I vow.

As I'm returning from the bathroom, I feel a hand on my shoulder.

"Hey, Brooke."

I spin to find Kevin behind me in the hall.

He's familiar, every inch of him, in a polished

shirt and tie with dress pants. The casual lunch-break version of his uniform at his father's law firm.

"What are you doing here?"

"It's your mom's event. My parents were the first to get an invite."

"You're not your parents."

"Maybe I came for you."

Emotions rise up that I swore I'd buried. He always had a way of making me feel special, even if his actions later proved otherwise.

"Kevin!" A voice calls from behind me, and we both look up.

The next moment, my brother's stepping between us, a glass of champagne in each hand. "I'd say it's great to see you, but we know that's not true."

Jay's smile widens and Kevin's falters.

"Nice to see you. Both of you." He heads back toward the main room, and I exhale.

"Tell me that's for me." I reach for the champagne before waiting for a response.

"Good work, acrobat," my brother says under his breath.

I have to win this contract, but if I'd thought it would be easy to ignore Kevin, I was wrong.

MILES

*O*ur next two games are on the road, and we could use a couple of wins.

We drop the first to a tough San Antonio team. Atlanta is up next.

They made some trades over the summer and came to play tonight. It starts out straightforward, but they home in on the fact we're short a big man, which means more defenders hanging around the perimeter to block every shot I put up.

I think about what Brooke said, that I'm not reaching my potential.

It got under my skin—or maybe that was her default mode of operating and I was already buzzing.

The attraction between us didn't surprise me,

but what did was how strong it was. I'm good at not taking things too seriously, but I've found myself thinking of her more than a few times this week.

"Miles!" Clay's glaring at me to keep my head in the game.

On the next play, the guy guarding me talks smack about my team.

The next time I get the ball, I'm out for blood.

It's Clay's and Rookie's job to play in the paint, up close. I'm the sniper. I watch and wait and stalk my prey from the outside, cutting through the other players to punk them, to line up the perfect shot...

I make the next three baskets with his hand in my face.

Brooke: Nice game.

The text comes through when I'm in the locker room.

Miles: I'm impressed you watched.

Brooke: One quarter.

Miles: What would it take to make you watch all four?

Brooke: I've got better things to do than watch a bunch of sweaty dudes run up and down a court.

We've been texting back and forth since our little shopping trip.

Mostly stuff to do with the reunion, but I saw a pic of her on social wearing one of the dresses I bought her.

Miles: Dress is fire btw.

Brooke: Thanks. I wore it to this event of my mom's. Something new is a good distraction from something broken.

Her words stuck with me on the plane, in shootaround the next day.

Is that what I do? Distract myself from what's broken with something shiny and new?

I'm still thinking about it when my phone jumps in my hand.

Aliya.

She hasn't texted since the party, and I'd figured she realized I wasn't worth the hassle.

"I've decided how you can make it up to me," she purrs when I answer. "Dinner from a private chef. Roses, at least six dozen, and—"

"This isn't working."

Silence floods the line, as if we're both surprised by what I've said. But now that I've started, I can't stop.

"I'm sorry if I didn't treat you the way I could have, but I was clear from the start. I'm not looking for a girlfriend. During the season I have to focus." I frown. "And maybe I have too many issues with—"

She hangs up before I can finish.

I'm still sitting in the ice bath when Jay and Clay come into the treatment room.

Jay grabs the tub next to mine, hissing as he sinks into it. "Figured you might be hooking up with someone after that game."

"My fan club is very active tonight on social."

"They leave a review of your performance?"

"I always get an A-plus."

Clay half grunts, half laughs as he claims the massage table in the corner.

The team's massage therapist appears a moment later to start working on his shoulders.

It's not a lie. I have a fan club. They have T-shirts and host meetings. I send them signed Christmas cards and stop by on Miles Day in the summer.

"Why do you look like you took a charge and still can't breathe?" Jay asks.

"You do," Clay offers from the massage table.

"Yeah? You can tell that with your view of the carpet?" I toss because he's face down.

Jay chuckles, the sounds ending with a tight exhale.

Never quite get used to the ice water.

The timer on my phone says I have another five minutes.

"I told this woman we're done hanging out," I say.

"Didn't think you were that into anyone."

"I wasn't. She wanted something I can't give her."

"You'd be surprised what you can give when you find the right person." Clay's voice is muffled by the headrest.

We were stunned when he met Nova and decided someone mattered as much as basketball.

"We can't all have your moody-broody thing sending out a signal to every girl in Colorado."

"The fuck are you talking about?"

Jay and I exchange a look. "You were begging for someone to see past the tattoos."

A grunt is our only response.

I chuckle. "I'm not looking for a person who completes me. I have a lot of friends."

Jay shifts in his tub. "It's different when you meet a woman who makes it so you never look at anyone else."

"You talking about..."

I almost say, "Chloe," but trail off. The massage therapist has heard a ton of shit, but it's better not to be talking about relationships with other people in the Kodiaks organization around, even though neither of them was with the club when they dated.

The idea of another person who sees you and laughs at your jokes and makes you smile, someone to take care of and go on adventures with is attractive.

But I know what it's like to lose people you thought were fixtures in your life.

This team is my family. They're everything to me.

Clay's propped up on his forearms, staring straight at me. "It'll happen when you're not looking. Most *inconvenient* fucking place. And her smile will light you up."

Brooke's face appears in my mind.

I agreed to be her fake date because I want her to know I have her back at that reunion. It's easier to look Jay in the eye and say his sister's going to be fine when I'm ensuring it myself.

And when she admitted to me about getting cut off by her family, I was incredulous on her behalf. I've had to live with the uncertainty of not knowing if you'd have enough, and I don't want her to feel that way.

I want to show her I care.

About her, about something.

And yeah, maybe I like having an excuse to be close to her.

Which is not what I signed up for, or what she did. She wanted someone to play the attentive date for this sorority reunion. Not someone to glaze over in practice imagining whether it's as much fun to argue with her naked as it is clothed.

I should be having her back in the daylight, not imagining all the things we could do in the dark.

"In the meantime, you have your pick of the

many ladies lined up outside for you," Jay tosses. "Lucky you."

"Yeah. Lucky me."

I dunk my head under the water. Maybe if I do it long enough, the cold will freeze my brain.

BROOKE

Rookie: Laser tag this weekend?

Jay: Hell yeah.

Clay: I'm too old for this shit.

Atlas: Ask Nova what she thinks.

Clay: Nova wants to know if Brooke's coming

Brooke: I could get out some aggression.

Clay: Then we're coming.

Rookie: You're so much more fun since you got married.

~

"*Y*ou're not so hard," I mutter as I click on my tablet and navigate to my online banking.

Part of the appeal of beautiful outfits and filters is that you don't have to look too hard at what's underneath.

I've been afraid to go through my finances with clear eyes and face up to what things really cost, but I need to understand.

Now, I'm perched at my marble kitchen island with a drip coffee as I scan through my expenses.

There's lots of travel. Dining out. But the biggest one is rent.

My two-bedroom apartment has been my happy place since I left college. My mom told me not to worry about the cost, so I didn't.

The thought of losing it is impossible. It's in a fabulous location, close to friends and shopping.

But as I compare my money coming in to

what's going out, it's increasingly obvious that I need to not only step up my game going forward, but I might need to make magic happen to cover rent for the next few months.

My chest constricts at the idea of having to give up the life I took for granted.

I'm still struggling when a knock comes at my door. I answer it to find the concierge there with a wrapped box.

As a creator, I get mailed stuff from brands, but this is different. Simple, wrapped in brown paper. I rip the paper off.

Inside is a pair of sparkly red Louboutins.

I pick up the shoes and examine them. I can see the spot where they were mended. It's barely visible, but it's there. They look as good as new. Maybe even better than new. The stitching is tighter, the crystals shine with a new luster.

The small card with them reads:

Bent but not broken.

– M

Miles did this. He had my shoes fixed after the party.

I'm surprised, grateful, and touched.

As I slip the shoes on, I feel a sense of warmth spreading through me.

It's such a small thing, but Kevin only made an effort when there was a public payoff, or if there was something in it for him.

This is a private detail that means the world.

I make my way back to the kitchen, my heels clicking on the tile as I whistle.

Last night, I caught the Kodiaks basketball game on TV. They were hosting a hungry Dallas team. Miles looked good out on the court. He was quick, agile, and his movements were fluid.

He's figuring out his shit. I can too.

I shift back onto the upholstered stool and return to my laptop.

First, I finish the seating arrangement so I can't help running into Elise.

I most definitely do not put Caroline and Kevin at our table.

Next, I pull together a mood board of ideas from Elise's teasers of the upcoming launch.

Scanning other social media, I look for connections in her brand and target market.

I asked a few friends about the budget Elise's

company would probably have to hire a spokesmodel, and they confirmed that it's big.

Exactly what I need to kick off the next phase of my life.

Which is why I review my social account with a careful eye, making sure I have the perfectly curated feed.

I can see which of the photos my mom's campaign didn't like.

To be safe, I archive them. Just temporarily.

I'm satisfied with my work and start to type a text to Miles.

Brooke: Thank you for the shoes. It was very thoughtful.

I'm about to hit Send when a new image shows up in my feed.

Judging from the angle, the picture of Aliya and Miles is a selfie taken with her phone, and posted with the caption "When you know..." with two heart emojis.

His arm is looped casually around her waist, and she's pressing close to him, her hand possessively on his neck.

It douses me in frigid water, like the icy pond at the gardens.

He said they weren't serious, but still, it's a reminder.

He's not really mine.

I stab the "unfollow" button—I only followed her in the first place because she's local, in the industry, and her campaigns occasionally give me inspiration.

But the sudden wave of nausea tells me it's no longer worth it.

Jay: Pick you up on the way to laser tag?

As I reach for my phone to reply to Jay, I see a message from Miles.

Miles: Need a ride to laser tag?

I shouldn't want to be alone in a car with Miles when a woman is posting cute pics of them on social.

My fingers hover over the keyboard.

Brooke: I'm going with Jay. I'll see you there.

When Jay and I arrive at the laser tag arena, Miles is waiting by his car in a white T-shirt and faded jeans, and he could be the boy next door.

If the boy next door had a wicked smile, A+ genes and a devout workout habit.

"Shit, I have to take this," Jay says, motioning to his ringing phone.

I shut the car door and start toward the building without him.

"Hey Princess," Miles says as I approach.

"Hi." I'm distracted enough I don't correct the nickname.

I stop a few feet away, trying to reestablish boundaries.

"How was your week?" His gaze searches mine.

"Good. Fine. Perfect." I force a smile I don't feel. "We should suit up."

We head into the arena and meet the others.

When I get inside, they're deciding house rules.

"Fouls are same as basketball," Rookie says.

"No way. The ref last night was way too tight

with his damn whistle. This is full contact. Retribution," says Atlas.

"Says the man with an injury who can't play," Jay notes.

Atlas frowns. "It's my shoulder. I can run fine."

"No one touch Atlas. We need him back yesterday." This is from Clay.

"You get the ref isn't here, right? You can't take him out." Rookie talks over Clay to Atlas.

"You realize we're not ten years old?" I taunt as I suit up.

"Maybe your girl should get a head start since she's so tiny," Jay says to Clay, glancing at Nova.

"My wife might be small but she's fast," Clay grunts.

Nova smiles sweetly and shoulders her rifle.

I feel Miles's eyes on me as we get ready, but as we strap on our gear for the game, anticipation builds in me.

I'm ready to kick some ass.

"Let's make it interesting," Jay suggests. "Loser buys dinner."

He names an expensive restaurant nearby.

The last thing I need is to pay for a pricey dinner, but I'm competitive.

We split up into teams. It's Atlas, Rookie,

Nova, and me. My brother has Miles, Chloe, Clay, and Sierra.

It's intense, and I find myself dodging and weaving through obstacles, trying to avoid getting hit by the laser beams.

I take out Chloe first. It's almost too easy.

My brother is my next target.

I'm excellent at hiding, but I have to run through an open area in pursuit of Jay.

Rookie's laughter catches me off guard. He's closing in.

I run into another figure and lose my balance, sprawling toward the floor, and the wind is knocked from my lungs when I hit the ground.

I gasp, but no sound comes out. It takes a minute for me to inhale normally, and when I do, I realize someone's on top of me.

He's straddling me, strong thighs on either side of my hips. His chest presses against my breasts, his warmth seeping through my clothing. His hand is on the floor next to my head.

"You all right?" Miles murmurs.

The walls around us are dark, the sound shrieking and laughter in the background. But in this second, the game feels far away.

"No thanks to you." My voice comes out like a

whisper. "Goddamn, you're heavy."

He rolls me so I'm on top in a move that's surprisingly agile.

"You're mad."

My pulse pounds as I try to collect my thoughts. I press the flat side of the rifle into his chest. "Are you going to shoot me, or is this chatting thing how you usually win at laser tag?"

Miles ignores my question. "Did they fix the shoes wrong?"

Dammit.

He shifts at the same time and my hand slips against his pec.

"They were fine. Better than fine." His concern only annoys me more. "And I'm not 'mad.'" I inhale roughly. "We're not kids."

I start to shift away but he rolls us once more so he's on top.

Miles leans over me. "Extremely aware of that right now, Princess."

There's the usual teasing in his voice, plus a charged edge that's new.

We're playing a game, but it's a different one from before.

My pulse doesn't slow.

"You and Aliya looked pretty 'more than

casual' on her socials."

The moment I say it, I feel exposed. More so than I do beneath Miles on the hard floor.

My rifle is trapped at my side and he's ignoring his. I squirm, trying to reach it but that only makes our good parts run distractingly.

"Aliya and I aren't anything. I ended it."

His words throw me even more than when he knocked me over.

"Why?"

Someone hoots in triumph.

"That was a cheap shot!" Nova wails in the distance.

My entire world is reduced to Miles's body, and mine.

"Like you said. Bigger things to think about this year, Princess."

I want to be annoyed with him, but my brain keeps repeating *they're not together* like a mantra.

He shifts back on his heels, pulling me up to sitting with him with a hand on the back of my neck, another on my waist.

Somehow my shirt has risen up.

Miles smooths down my hair. His thumb brushes my jaw, careless and perfect.

I arch into his touch in the dark. A whimper

escapes my throat before I can stop it.

Miles's hand stills.

Fuck.

He totally heard that. Felt my response.

So much for trying to appear unaffected.

Hollering in the background splits the darkness as the Kodiaks search one another out.

The sound of footsteps running nearby enters my ears.

"B, get up! I've got you!" Atlas is behind me, crowing.

Everything happens fast. Miles's vest lights up, and he groans in defeat as he falls back.

Atlas helps me up and high-fives me once I'm standing. "Hell yes!"

We won.

I turn and offer Miles a hand up. He takes it, nearly pulling me over as he uses it for leverage to rise.

His hand lingers in mine.

"Good game," he says next to my ear.

My hand tingles.

I don't know what game we're playing anymore.

All the way through dinner, I find my attention lingering on Miles across the table, grinning and making everyone laugh.

I'm still thinking about the sensation of having his hard body against mine. How I got caught up in the moment, gave myself up to how good his hands felt touching me.

It was barely a touch. The guy fixed my shoes and tackled me to the ground and I'm suddenly hornier than I have been in months.

The stress is getting to me. I clearly need to blow off some steam. A little me time with a vibrator or two, maybe some light porn, and I'll be a whole new woman.

When the bill comes, he's the first to reach for it.

I fall into step with Nova on our way outside, talking about her plans for a new art exhibit.

"Hey, Brooke." We glance back as Miles catches up to us.

He shrugs under his jacket, a lingering grin on his face from the round of jokes and ribbing inside.

Clay loops an arm around his wife, and they

break off with the others. I glance back only to realize everyone's out ahead of us.

"I was thinking about this sorority thing." Miles pulls the collar of his jacket up. "It's one thing if you have a date, but it's better if you have a boyfriend."

"A boyfriend?" I echo.

"Yeah. A serious one. You want to put on a good show in front of these sisters, then let's go all the way."

My mouth drops open.

"You want to be my fake boyfriend." It sounds even crazier out loud.

"Why not?"

I laugh. "I have a lot riding on this, Miles. And you're not capable of that kind of deception."

"Act like I'm in head over heels for you? Like I have been for a while?" His smile is heart-stoppingly sexy. "Game on, Princess."

13

BROOKE

"*T*he chair coverings should be cream, not ecru. The resort said they didn't have any in stock. Can you believe it?" Caroline demands.

The Zoom call to go over last-minute sorority weekend planning was supposed to be over ages ago. I've already done what I said I would do. Now, they're going through every tiny detail.

Kill me.

Brooke: I can't believe you dodged Caroline's planning call.

Ruby: I was performing emergency

surgery on an eighteen-year-old kid who impaled himself on a bong.

Brooke: You're a lucky bitch.

I turned my video off to sift through the piles of designer clothes I dragged out of my wardrobe so I can find some pieces to sell until I get this contract.

But as I go through one dress and bag after another, it's hard to identify any I could bear to part with. I have amazing memories of all of them, ideas of ways I haven't worn them yet.

"Brooke, are you even listening?" Caroline's voice interrupts my thoughts.

I click on my video, tilting the camera so it's not obvious I'm on the floor surrounded by clothes. "Sorry, what?"

"I said, can you confirm the table chart for meals?"

"It's done. I've emailed it over."

"Good. Hannah was supposed to do it, but she's been a flake."

I frown. "I thought she was pulling eighty-hour weeks at her firm?"

"Everyone has an excuse." Caroline sighs,

nodding as she scans something on her screen next to the camera. "That's it."

I'm ready to hang up when she adds, "Brooke, would you stay on the line with me?"

The others click off, and it's just the two of us.

"Listen, I'm not sure how to say things so I'll just say it." Her thick lash extensions blink. "I'm bringing Kevin to the reunion."

"I see." I don't let on that I already knew, but I'm glad I did.

"I know you dated for two years"—four, actually—"and you were completely obsessed with him. I don't want it to be weird."

My brows lift. "I was never obsessed with him, Caroline. We grew up together, and it ended."

In truth, the idea of the two of them makes me slightly nauseated, but I'm not about to admit it.

Her lips pinch together, and she plays with her hair. "I think it's getting serious, or I wouldn't bring him. Because sisterhood comes first."

"Great," I say. "Just so we're clear, I'm speaking to Elise about her brand sponsorship."

"You are?"

"I know you're probably in the running too, but you'd care way too much about sisterhood to let this get in the way."

Caroline nods, but I see the doubt in her eyes. "We don't need any drama during the reunion."

"I'm a big girl. I can handle seeing my ex."

She smiles. "I know you can. No matter what mess you land in, you bounce right back."

My hand forms a fist, manicured nails digging into my palm.

She's talking about what happened at the end of junior year.

"Is there anything else you wanted to discuss?" I ask tightly.

She shakes her head. "No, I think that's everything. Thanks again, Brooke. You're a lifesaver."

"Miles and I will see you at the reunion."

"You mean Miles Garrett, that basketball player you had a crush on through college?"

My finger hovers over the "Call End" button.

"When you were dating Kevin," she goes on slyly, "we always thought you secretly liked Miles."

Surprise jolts me. "He was in the NBA when we were in school."

"Sure, but he used to come around." She laughs, a tinkling sound. "Don't get your panties in a twist. It's cute you're still chasing after Miles after all these years. Why haven't I seen any pictures of you?"

"We're keeping it on the down-low."

Her slow smile is predatory. "Maybe there's something to jocks after all. I mean, they get a free ride through school, and they don't even have to get good grades."

My fingers brush one of the piles of clothes and land on the Louboutins Miles had fixed for me.

"Seems to me that while most people we knew were milking family contacts or popping pills to get into law school, Miles figured out how to make millions a year with his hands." I turn the shoe between my fingers. "They're big hands too. Compared to every guy I've dated before, he definitely has enormous... hands. I'll see you at the reunion," I say breezily, ending the call.

Her pretty face freezes in a satisfying O before the image disappears.

That was a load of performative bullshit. But I'm most annoyed over her dig about Miles. He's smart and funny and kind and talented, and he gets what's important. More than most of the guys I went to school with. Definitely more than Kevin.

Did I have a crush on him in college?

Sure, I stared at him when he took me for

151

pancakes, imagined what it might be like if he kissed me.

More than kissed me.

I blame it on hormones and being twenty and sexually adventurous.

I flop onto my bed and pull out my phone.

Brooke: Caroline wanted to know if I was cool with her bringing Kevin.

Ruby: And of course you are.

Brooke: The coolest. Wait, why am I the coolest?

Ruby: Because you're bringing this man.

She sends through a picture and... *Hello*.

Evidently, he did an underwear campaign. How did I not know about this?

He's shot on a dark backdrop, lounging back in a chair. In another picture, he's lying on his side.

Ruby: You failed to mention he was an underwear model, Little Sis.

I've heard they stuff boxer briefs for shoots like that.

If they don't... I have no clue what's in there or how it would fit in me or any other woman.

I suddenly want to find out.

Every ridge of his abs is decadent. But it's the expression on his face, as though he's looking straight at me, into me, that does me in.

I'm thinking about him on top of me at laser tag, how hard and strong he felt.

I do a search and find more pictures. Heat spreads through me as I stare at the screen.

His chiseled features and toned body are unreal.

How he looks is nothing compared to how he feels.

Truth is, I've been thinking about it ever since he tackled me at laser tag.

"Act like I'm in head over heels for you? Like I have been for a while? Game on, Princess."

For a moment, I imagine how it would've felt if he'd meant it. Having him stake his claim on me, those blue eyes turning possessive.

Even if it's fake, I can still acknowledge our chemistry. Especially since Aliya is out of the picture.

Because fighting it is killing me.

I ditch the computer and reach toward the bedside table for my vibe. I keep my phone open to one of the pictures as I close my eyes and imagine my fingers running over Miles's chiseled stomach.

My heart beats faster.

I think about his abs, his tongue, his hands.

My hand moves slowly down my stomach, pushing down my panties. I tuck my vibrator between my legs and press it to my clit.

The vibration is on low, and I press the button to raise it a notch. My hips buck toward it. Toward him.

I think about his warm breath against my neck.

How he felt over me.

My fingers push inside me, working my clit and teasing my entrance at the same time.

I imagine how it would feel to have him drag me down, rake his lips across mine. Grind his hips against me, make me feel how hard he is everywhere.

In the dark, with a little more time, he could have slid his fingers down my pants. Made me ride his hand until I came.

I lean back, pressing the vibe harder against my clit.

In my mind, Miles is lying over me, his cock deep inside me. Those blue eyes are hot with want.

My hips move faster, my fingers sliding into my pussy. I'm so wet and so turned on and so frustrated that I can barely think.

I hit the button again for another gear.

The toy doesn't respond.

I lift it away for a moment, and a blinking light alerts me to a low battery.

No, no, no.

I bury it back between my legs and focus on the vibration that's left.

I picture him thrusting. How good he'd feel, the scent of his skin, the low rasp of his voice as he said my name.

My neck arches back, my legs trembling.

The vibe dies.

No fucking way.

My phone rings and I jump.

It's him.

"You sound weird," Miles says when I answer the phone on the fourth ring. "What, did I interrupt you getting off to me?"

I hit mute long enough to scream into a pillow, then drop the exhausted vibe in the bedside table like a dirty secret and slam the drawer.

"Princess? Still there?"

I press unmute and take a steadying breath. "Just finished a call on last-minute sorority business before the weekend."

"Like flaunting your incredible boyfriend?"

"Naturally."

"So... why aren't you gloating?"

Because my vibe quit and I was five seconds from a really great orgasm.

I lift a shoulder even though he can't see. "Caroline's being Caroline. She has a problem with anyone who doesn't do things exactly the way she would." I think of her comments about Hannah.

Hannah, who nearly single-handedly organized a dozen events for us throughout school, who was the first to offer help with a smile or a shoulder to cry on.

"Why are you friends with them?"

I catch my own eye in the mirror over my dresser. "At the time, it seemed like a great idea. I never had sisters. It was like a guaranteed friend group."

"Like a basketball team."

"No. A basketball team's only good as long as you're winning." I flop onto my back and hug a pillow to my chest.

My mind drifts back to Caroline's skepticism about Miles. "Anyway, we have one issue."

"Which is?"

"If we're supposed to be dating, it's going to look like it came out of nowhere when we show up together. It's too convenient."

"So, we have to sell it when we get there."

"Or…" I shift onto an elbow. "If we sell it ahead of time, it'll take less convincing next weekend."

"What do you mean?"

A hint of guilt rises up, and I brush it away. "The girls will understand if we're trying to keep things under the radar, but I need to have a few pictures of the two of us. Otherwise, it's weird. I don't have to post them publicly, but one in the reunion thread would help."

"Pics of us doing what?"

I have an image of me lying next to him in that advertisement, him wearing only boxer briefs. Those blue eyes staring into my soul in that unnerving way they do. Me straddling him, feeling him between my thighs. Miles grabbing the back of my head, his fingers tangled in my hair as he drags me—

I clear my throat and click into Pinterest, searching for cute couple's photoshoots.

"Something like this." I download couple cute ideas and send them. "Did you get them?"

"Just came through."

There's a pause, and for a heart-stopping second, I swear he's going to call bullshit.

"Let's do it. Tonight," he says.

I roll onto my side. In the mirror, my brows are high on my face. "Wait. Don't you have a game?"

The Kodiaks are hosting visitors in a high-stakes game.

"Come watch me play. We'll meet up after."

Watch me play.

Not the Kodiaks. Not my brother.

My stomach does a little flip.

I hang up and drop the phone on the bed.

It's barely a minute before I slide my hand down my stomach again, no vibrator required.

I might be a teeny bit for real into my fake boyfriend...

Because the echo of, *"Come watch me play,"* is all it takes.

14

BROOKE

"I can't believe you came!" Nova gushes as she runs across the parking garage toward me, her sister, Mari, on her heels.

"What do you mean?" I prompt when she releases me from a hug.

"You haven't been to a game since finals."

I'm here because Miles and I are taking pics after, but I was happy I said yes the moment I texted Nova to see if she was going.

It's been a busy week without much friend time since the café.

My excitement has nothing to do with my fake boyfriend inspiring a very real, very all-star-worthy orgasm, or that I'd like to watch him play in person.

When we get inside the building, it's energetic chaos.

I forgot how intense the fan base is. BEARFORCE shirts are everywhere, the team's purple-and-gold colors painted across everything from faces to flags to gear.

We strip off our jackets. Nova's wearing Clay's jersey. It's cute, her pink hair skimming along the purple fabric and brushing the "WADE" in capital letters along the back.

"You're not wearing a jersey," I tell Mari as we walk the private hallways toward the team VIP box.

"Harlan doesn't have one," she says.

"The GM should get a number," Nova decides as we head into the box.

I've watched games from here, and by watched, I mean worked on my phone or flirted with bartenders, with the exception of the finals last year when I genuinely paid a little attention.

Nova and Mari go out front to the seats and I follow.

The arena is packed. The roar of the crowd surges as another wave of Kodiaks fans flow into their rows.

We're there in time for the player announcements, and I watch the starters run out.

It's dark in the stands. No one can see me, so I let my gaze run over Miles. My eyes linger on his body, shown off to perfection in that uniform.

The guy works on his body as a full-time job. I'm simply acknowledging it with my respectful ogling, as his very temporary, very fake, very serious girlfriend.

"There a reason you're eye-fucking him more than normal?" Nova asks innocently.

"Hmm?" I ask as I sip my wine. "We're practicing. I'm bringing him to the sorority thing as my date. Fake date."

My friend grabs my arm, fingers digging into my flesh. "I knew something was up. I leave for a few days and everything is upside down." She sighs. "This is how it starts."

"Nothing starts. It's all for show to help me land this brand deal with Elise."

"So, you can't picture climbing him like a redwood?"

Heat starts low in my spine. A warmth I can't entirely pin on the excitement from the game has my lips and fingertips humming.

"His gorgeous eyes? That mouth? The messy hair?" Nova says each word as though she's building a tantalizing fire of reasons, one log at a time.

"You're married, Mrs. Wade," I remind her with a laugh.

"I'm just saying. He's charming, charismatic. I wouldn't blame you for wondering. And you'll be with him the entire weekend. Talking. Flirting. Dancing. Tell me there'll be dancing..."

"This weekend is about the girls," I say, trying to steer the conversation away from Miles. "Not the guys."

"Well, he's watching you too," she says sweetly.

My head snaps toward the court. His gaze locks on mine, and I feel the air flow from my lungs. He tilts his chin in my direction, and the corners of his lips lift into a little smirk.

Gah. I'm so screwed.

The first quarter starts, and the competition comes out strong, taking it down the court to the basket, playing hard. The Kodiaks are a step slow by comparison.

Mari's not as into it as Nova, who mutters on every play.

"Come on, Clay." Her hand grips mine.

"How's his knee?" I ask Nova.

"Good so far this season. But it's early."

Clay's an all-star, but he's had some serious injuries in the past—ones that cost him professionally and personally.

I squeeze her hand.

It's back and forth, the Kodiaks falling behind by a basket. Then two. Then another.

Nova and I exchange worried looks.

"Come on, Kodiaks!" Nova cheers, jumping up and down.

My eyes sweep over the crowd. Almost all of them are on their feet, screaming. I glance back at the court. The team is getting frustrated.

I stand and holler, "Come on, Kodiaks!"

Miles's attention cuts toward me, brows lifting in surprise.

"Good job, Kodashian," Nova whispers.

Jay brings the ball up the court, passes it to Clay. He cuts into the paint, then turns and fires it out to Miles, who's along the baseline, but the defense is there, guarding him.

My breath catches.

"Shoot over him," I mutter.

"Miles won't make it," Nova worries. "You know how many blocks the other guy has?"

The shot clock ticks down. It would be so easy

to release the ball, to get desperate and fire. Miles rises up to shoot.

I'm already dreading it. Except...

It's not a shot. It's a pump fake designed to make the defender lunge for him.

Only when the defender crashes into Miles does he put the shot up. The whistle shrills. *Foul.*

Hell yes.

Miles sinks all three from the free-throw line. I feel each of them as if I'm putting up the shots myself.

On the third shot, he looks up at me with a wink.

I bite my lip.

When the whistle blows to signal halftime, the Kodiaks lead by one.

"I'm going up to see Harlan," Mari says, rising.

"Do they bang on his desk at the break?" I ask Nova.

"Probably. She leaves every time." She shifts forward, eyes dancing with mischief. "So, how exactly does this fake date thing work? You sleep in the same bed, slather on the PDA for your adoring public, and make up nicknames for each other?"

"I've requested two beds, the goal is adoring looks and the occasional forehead kiss, and technically, he already has a nickname for me," I state, and Nova gasps.

"What does he call you?"

"Princess. It's bullshit, and I'm going for snacks," I add before she can comment.

I leave the box and find myself wandering into the main hallway packed with fans.

Normally, I don't notice what everyone is wearing—it's a sea of purple and yellow—but tonight, it's as if all I see are Miles jerseys.

Especially on women, I notice as I head toward the concession stands.

I find myself in line behind a group of women a few years older.

"Who's the hottest?" one says to another.

"Clay."

"No way. It's Miles. I'd bang him any day."

I stare holes in the back of her jersey as the girls order their food and head toward their seats.

I order a beer and two bags of popcorn, which I have to juggle on the way back. The Kodiaks store is in my peripheral vision, my attention lingering on his jersey, displayed front and center.

"Ooh, what did you buy?" Nova asks when I reappear next to her, dropping into the seat with my snacks.

The second half starts, and Miles is fire. I love it when he gets what he wants.

They squeak out the win, and the building goes crazy.

I go a little crazy too.

We're seeking spokesmodels! Think you have what it takes to rep the brand? Tag us over the next month for your chance at a major collaboration.

The notification from Elise's company account pops up as I'm heading down to find Miles.

My pulse accelerates.

It's confirmation that she's looking for a partnership, but it means everyone else will be applying too.

I need to stay focused on my mission.

When I get to the hallway outside the locker room, Miles is leaning against the wall, checking his phone. He's freshly showered, hair falling across his forehead, dark lashes over lowered eyes as he scans the screen.

It's worth the crowd of admirers I had to battle just to get to security and wave my VIP pass.

He straightens the moment he spots me.

"You didn't get distracted and hook up with anyone after the game?" I ask, shoving my hands in the pockets of my coat.

He lifts a shoulder. "You either."

I glance around. "I don't see a line of people who want to fuck *me* tonight."

"Because I got rid of them."

"You wouldn't." I can't stop the laughter that bubbles up.

His gaze flicks over me, his smug mouth lifting at the corner. "Careful, Princess. I *will* obliterate the competition for your fake heart."

Before I can process the words, Nova comes up behind me.

"Hey, you. I'm the designated photographer for this evening."

Miles looks between us, and for a second, I think he's disappointed.

"I told Nova about our plan," I supply.

"Right." He shakes his head and hitches a thumb down the hall. "I had a place in mind."

He leads the way out a side door and into the street. We walk a few blocks, blending in with the little bit of foot traffic remaining more than an hour after the game.

Nova's smiling as she trails just behind, texting Clay to let him know she'll meet him later to blow his grumpy dick or whatever they're into.

We get to a restaurant, and he shows us up the side steps, waiting for Nova and me to go first. The door opens out onto a rooftop with fairy lights strewn all around.

"Pretend I'm not even here," Nova says as she steps a few feet away, finding her favorite lighting.

"Right." Miles rocks on his heels as if he's on edge.

Unlikely. Nothing freaks this guy out.

"If we're going to sell that we're dating seriously, we should discuss things we'd know about one another," he says.

"Such as?" I'm surprised he came this prepared, especially when he reaches into his pocket for a folded piece of paper.

"I have a list of questions."

"You printed that out from the internet."

"Yup. What's your biggest dream?"

Click. The camera phone goes off. I'm aware of Nova moving around us.

"Pass."

"You can't pass on the first question." He laughs.

"Sure I can. How many real couples know what the other person's biggest dream is? What you truly want is like a big flashing light pointing to your motivations and your weaknesses."

"Never thought about it like that." He turns it over. "My dream is to play on the USA men's basketball team."

"Why?" His answer surprises me. "You don't even get paid to do it."

Click. Click.

"That's exactly why. You're playing for pride with the best guys in the country. You do it because you love it. It's hard as hell to get a spot."

Click. Click.

"You want to be the best, then."

"Nah. I want to be good enough to play side by side with the best."

"That's the same thing."

"Is it?"

"Next question," I say, still thinking about his answer.

"What's one thing only your friends know about you."

I take a breath. "I have a wild side."

Miles leans in, his eyes sparkling with curiosity. "Tell me."

"I've always been drawn to the danger and excitement of things like skydiving and bungee jumping."

"Why?"

I turn it over. "Probably because Jay used to get lots of attention playing basketball. At first, I did it for the attention, and my mother was horrified. Eventually, I realized I liked it. I like being somewhere I'm free and feel alive."

"Huh," Miles says, his voice low with appreciation. "You're even braver than I thought."

The way he looks at me, with a mixture of admiration and something else, makes me feel like I could conquer the world.

"Ooh, that's good," Nova says. "Get closer. Miles, put your arms around her."

Miles pulls me to him, his arms snaking around my waist. I feel his breath on my neck as he nuzzles into me. The warmth of his body against mine sends a shiver down my spine.

We go through the list as Nova takes picture after picture, our bodies pressed close together, our faces mere inches apart.

Is he as affected by this as I am?

We're supposed to be building evidence for our fake relationship, but nothing about his touch feels forced.

"What's your biggest fear?" I ask.

"Pass."

"Really?" I cock my head. "You're afraid it'll come true if you say it out loud?"

"Something like that." His lips curve.

I feel the heat of his breath on my lips, and I know I should pull away, but I can't. I turn to say something, but his mouth is right fucking there.

I'm trying to keep focused, but it's taking everything in me.

"I need to call Clay," Nova says, reminding me we're not alone. "See if he can pick me up."

She waves and heads for the other side of the rooftop.

"You got us a chaperone?" Once she's out of earshot, Miles' voice, low and husky, makes me turn.

"A photographer," I correct.

The sound he makes is somewhere between a groan and a laugh. "Because you don't think you can keep your hands off me."

I scoff. The ego on this man.

"Did you like watching me play?" Miles changes the subject.

"I like it better when you play the way you did tonight," I reply. "You were good. You took no prisoners."

He folds his arms, a slow grin spreading across his face. "You keep this up, you're going to become a Kodashian. I'll have to get you in my jersey."

I mumble something.

"Didn't catch that."

I huff out a sigh. "I said I already have your jersey."

Miles's smug smile fades. His usual playfulness twists into a new intensity. "Where exactly is this jersey of mine that you own?"

"In my closet. Where the clothes live."

"Interesting." He draws out the word.

"There were hundreds—probably thousands—of women wearing your jersey tonight," I say, pretending I'm not fascinated by the predatory way he stalks toward me.

"Only one I care about right now, Princess."

My body responds to his closeness, my skin erupting in goosebumps. When his hand grabs my waist, my nipples harden.

"I'm going to need to see you in that."

His thumb rubs a slow circle against my hip that makes me ache.

"You're better at this than I thought," I manage.

"At what?"

I slant him a look from under my lashes. "Pretending."

His eyes are blue fire. "You have no idea how good I can be."

Nova's two dozen feet away, chatting with her husband, but it feels like just Miles and me here.

Damn, it would be so easy to admit how affected I am by his electric blue eyes, the humor he wears like a hoodie, the edge underneath that always seems to come out when I'm around.

"I'm glad I chose you for this," I hear myself say.

Miles rubs a hand over his jaw. "You chose me, huh?"

"Yeah. Instead of one of the other guys I could have invited to this Kappa reunion." I smile. "Because then it would've been more like an actual date," I explain, "and it's hard to find someone you can spend the weekend with who'll act like a gentleman in front of your sorority sisters, and who you also want to fuck—or you don't want to fuck, and they're cool with that..."

Nova returns, saving me from whatever Miles's reaction was. "Clay's coming in ten. I have time for a few more, if you want?"

"I think we have lots," I say at the same time Miles says, "What about dialing up the PDA?"

We both turn to him, surprised.

Nova's tapping a finger against her chin. "I like it. Brooke?"

I lift a shoulder, as if the idea of us turning this up a notch doesn't affect me.

"You were the one who wanted pics to prove we're for real," he says. "Let's leave no question in their minds."

But as Miles leans in, inching closer, my heart hammers. Nova says something, but I don't hear her.

We're so close. We've been a breath apart before, we've even touched in a casual way, but this is different.

He's completely locked in. If my pulse skipped and my palms got sweaty—kind of like they're doing now—I swear he'd notice.

His lips brush mine.

All I see are stars. Not the ones overhead, but the ones behind my closed eyes.

He's firm and confident, his mouth parting mine like he's done it a thousand times before.

As if he couldn't care less about the camera angle or who's watching.

Electricity sings along my nerves, lighting me up everywhere.

I knew we had chemistry, but this is something else. It's physics, a damned gravitational pull dragging us together, insisting that his mouth on mine is the natural order of things.

All I hear is the buzzing in my ears, Miles's rough intake of breath the moment before his fingers sink into my hair. My hips are flush against his through our clothes—probably because he's got a hand on my waist, holding me in place under his mouth, his thumb stroking right above my hipbone.

This better look good, I think hazily, *because it feels fucking fantastic.*

Honking from somewhere down at street level makes me pull away.

Nova hands back the phone, fanning herself. "Clay's here. Excuse me while I go jump my husband." She wiggles her fingers and shoots me a look before heading toward the stairs.

I watch her disappear and feel Miles's eyes on my back.

"Think we got enough to convince your Kappas?" he asks lightly.

His phone rings, splitting the silence.

"Shit. It's my grandma." He answers, turning away.

A moment later he returns, pocketing the phone.

"I need to see her. I can drop you off first."

It sounds urgent. I don't want him to lose time on my account.

"Take me with you?"

MILES

"Hey, Grams," I say after knocking and pushing open the door a crack.

She's not in her chair in the living room.

I cross her suite, heading for the light in her bedroom.

Grams is in bed, fully dressed, blankets tugged up around her waist, with a pen in hand and a crossword book in her lap.

"Miles." She lifts her gaze to me, her expression sharp as she sets the book down.

When I was growing up, she was active and strong. Always looking out for me and bandaging my scraped knees and tsking over bruises I picked up on the court. She looks small.

"Tip-off was early. Thought I'd stop by." I hug her carefully. "You want to tell me what happened?"

"I was practicing my dancing and lost my balance."

"The staff said they found you on the floor."

Her snort is delicate. "They certainly did not."

I pull a chair up to her bed. "Is your walker around?"

"Who did you bring?" Grams calls, dodging the question.

I forgot to introduce Brooke. Only because when I'm with Grams, I'm trying hard to pay attention to how she's doing, what she needs. I'm not naturally a details person, but with her I have to be.

Brooke pokes her head in, a wide smile on her face. "Hi, I'm Brooke. I like your place."

Grams starts to get out of bed, and Brooke waves a hand. "Please, don't make a fuss for me."

"It's no fuss. I've been resting too long."

She starts across the floor, and I follow behind her as she moves toward the coffee table.

It's two steps before the chair that she wobbles.

"Sure you wouldn't feel better with the

walker?" I try, nodding to the corner where the device sits facing the wall like a child in time-out.

"You would. Not me."

Brooke nods toward the Monopoly game spread out on the table. "Let me guess, you're the thimble?"

"I'm the terrier," I say.

Brooke grins. "You're a couple moves away from victory."

"That's not the point," I say.

"It's not?"

"We've been playing this game for... a few months?"

"Since the summer," Grams confirms.

"Tell me about this dance you're going to," Brooke says.

Grams launches into a description and how she used to love dancing.

"I used to dance as a kid," Brooke offers. "The right shoes made all the difference. What shoes do you wear?"

"Oh, just these slippers." Grams gestures to the satin slip-ons on her feet.

"There are some amazing shoes with grippy soles." Brooke pulls out her phone, the one with the cracked screen, and navigates to a page.

"Goodness."

"What size are you, a seven?" Brooke eyes up Grams's feet.

"That's right."

She clicks a few buttons. "They'll be at your door in a few days," Brooke confirms.

My chest twinges with gratitude.

Brooke is good with Grams, making her laugh and smile. I see the kindness and empathy in her eyes.

I knew she was a great friend, but her care is blowing my mind right now.

We spend a while longer chatting with Grams, until I'm confident she's as all right as she says.

"Doctor's going to check you out for that fall tomorrow," I say as we stand.

"It's not necessary."

"My friend Ruby is a doctor. She says she loves seeing patients when there's nothing broken. It makes her day," Brooke offers.

Grams laughs. "I'll keep that in mind."

We say goodbye and head for the door.

"Thank you," I say as we leave my grandmother's room and start down the hall together. "For everything."

Brooke waves me off. "The shoes weren't expensive."

It's not about the money, I want to say.

"This place used to be better." I notice once again the lack of staff as we leave. Frustration rises up, and I take a deep breath. "She's done so much for me, and I hate the idea that she doesn't have everything she wants."

I can't be here for my grandmother all the time, no matter how much she needs me. I'll never repay what she did for me.

Brooke hooks her pinkie in mine. "You're doing great."

It's a simple touch, but she doesn't pull back as we walk side by side, me adjusting my strides to her shorter ones.

I open the passenger door for her and she shifts inside. I round to the driver's side and get in.

"Miles?" she says as I fasten my seatbelt.

"Yeah?" I stare through the windshield.

"When I said you didn't care enough about anything... I was wrong."

Her eyes are soft and full of understanding. I can feel my walls crumbling down as she looks at me with such acceptance.

I'm surrounded by guys every day I care about, but sometimes I feel completely alone.

I look at her.

Really look at her.

The shadows falling across her face make her seem younger and more vulnerable.

It shouldn't be appealing, but she fucking calls to me.

She leans across the console and brushes her mouth over mine.

Time stops.

Brooke's scent is warm and floral. Her lips are soft and determined.

The brush of her skin on mine, the way her fingers slide into my hair as she shifts closer, the tiniest sigh—they're pieces of an addictive puzzle I never asked to play.

But I can't stop.

I lean across the console and drag her toward me on a groan.

Her breasts crush against my chest. Her mouth parts as I kiss her back.

She tastes sweet. Dangerous. The way she meets me with every touch...she isn't starstruck. When her hand presses against my chest, it's like she owns me.

I want seconds and thirds. Want to go back to her every damned moment for more.

My greedy fingers sink into her hips, my other hand tangled in her hair.

The Range Rover normally feels spacious, but right now I'm furious with how cramped we are. Every time I try to shift, my elbow is blocked by the seat. When I pull her closer, the console acts as a barrier.

I want to pull her into my lap and feel her body the way I barely got the chance to at laser tag.

"Miles," Brooke whispers against my mouth.

There's something in her voice that's as much a warning as it is a seduction.

She's kissing me like she cares and wants me to care too. Like it's not only desire, but feelings.

I can't give her that, no matter how much I want to.

I tug her back an inch. "Princess... I can't do this."

Brooke stiffens against me. Her expression transforms, the softness gone, replaced with surprise, then coolness.

Then she's back on the other side of the car and fastening her seatbelt.

Shit. This is exactly what I didn't want—for her to feel rejected.

"Brooke, wait."

"We should get going."

Her voice is resolved, and it's clear this conversation is over.

I debate arguing with her but end up putting the car into gear to drive her home.

BROOKE

"*Y*ou ever consider yoga?" Nova puffs, her pink ponytail bobbing and her earmuffs making her look like a kid.

"Too slow," I say as the trail turns. My legs power me higher, the leaves crunching under my feet. My lungs burn from the exertion and cool air as we stop at a lookout point with a waterfall.

Nova oohs and aahs over the sight.

"You should paint it," I suggest.

"Not lugging my supplies this far up," she counters.

I grab my water bottle, chugging gratefully.

"So, you looked pretty close with Miles last night," my friend says.

The images she sent me documenting our fake romance flash through my mind.

Us laughing.

Him holding me.

Finally, one in which Miles's lips were pressed to mine.

"We had to make it look convincing," I say.

Nova's smile is wide and genuine. "Well, you definitely convinced me."

Me too.

My body heats with the memory of how it felt to take those pictures, how natural every move and touch seemed.

"We kind of hooked up in his car," I admit, and my friend claps her hands in delight.

"Tell me it was life affirming."

"It was good," I groan. "Until he shut it down."

"Maybe it threw him? When I started dating Clay, he was totally closed off. But it was only because he was so used to everyone wanting things from him, expecting him to be a certain way."

I never suspected Miles could be so committed to anything.

Anyone.

But seeing him with his grandmother proved that idea wrong.

It had me questioning how much of him is the way he acts in public and how much is real.

Blurring that line is the fact that I kissed him.

He obviously decided it was a bad idea because he pulled back, cool as anything, as if it was all part of the game.

"I've never had a guy look out for me the way Miles does. I'm not sure what to think of it," I say.

"Not even Kevin?"

"Especially not Kevin," I snort.

We start our descent down the trail, the leaves crunching under our feet.

"You never told me what happened with him," Nova says.

I'm almost grateful for the distraction from Miles as I swipe the back of my neck, at the sweat collecting under the collar of my Lululemon top.

"He came from an important family that donated to my mom's campaign. My mom loved that we were dating. We were an 'it' couple on campus, everyone going out of their way to include us. Until one of my sorority sisters was going through my room and found—well, let's say it's something that violated sorority rules and school ones."

"It can't have been that bad." Nova frowns.

"It was." A pang of regret rises up at the memories I've always tried to downplay. "My name got raked through the mud. My mom covered for me. She made a contribution to the school, and they agreed to let it slide. I talked to Kevin about it, we got on the same page, and I thought it went away.

"A week later, Kevin dumped me by text. He said I wasn't the person he thought I was." The back of my throat tastes bitter. "We were supposed to go to a big party that night to celebrate the end of exams. Instead, I spent the night in my room trying to reach him. He never got back to me. I didn't see him all summer, and he avoided me the next semester."

"I'm so sorry."

"It was a long time ago. I was young and stupid."

"Feelings are strange like that. Just when you think they're in the past, you get triggered and they're fresh."

I wish she was wrong. "If only I could take out the part of me that lived through that. The part of me that cared so damn much."

"Yeah, but then you wouldn't be you, and I love you." She hooks an arm around my shoulders.

"You know, this weekend could be the perfect time to come to peace with it."

I laugh. "Peace is a strange word to apply to college."

My friend's eyes glint. "Even so. It does seem like a big coincidence that everything's coming back together at once, doesn't it?"

MILES

"Huh. New max," Rookie says as I finish my leg press.

I grunt. "Better be."

Rookie nods for me to swap out with him for his set. My thighs shake as I rise and step out, letting him work in as I reach for my water bottle and chug the contents.

We're on the road for two games this week. After last week's positive momentum, we dropped the first one. It felt like a setback, though no one's saying it out loud.

"Shooting guard tomorrow had thirty-five points last night," Jay comments.

"Miles will crush him tomorrow. Right?" Rookie asks.

"Uh-huh," I say absently as I open my socials.

There are too many comments to respond to today. Lots of women, including a few in my DMs from the city I'm visiting.

Busy, I start to type.

But the truth is... I don't want to.

I click into the pics of me and Brooke that Nova sent me this morning with a text saying, *You should look at these.*

Never understood the impulse girls have to take pics, to obsess over them, but I've looked at these half a dozen times.

Maybe more.

One frame after another of us close, me touching her, her smiling at me.

We look good together.

She's beautiful, smart, and funny. She sees another side of me, one I've never thought too hard about.

But it's one thing to play a game with her. It's another to be so consumed by her I can't think of anyone else, to think that she might be the prize.

I've got a lot of casual friends, but letting

someone in close is a big deal. They leave, there's a hole in your heart.

Brooke's worked her way in.

I want Brooke Ellis.

There, I said it.

Since she asked me to be her fake boyfriend, my cock is always hard, my brain is useless, and the way she looks at me like she could either fuck me or eviscerate me is my Roman Empire.

She's the one setting all the ground rules, but *she* kissed *me*.

Her perfect body was over mine and I could have easily worked off her pants, been inside her in that car in under a minute.

I know because I've pictured it a thousand damned times since.

Problem is, she's not some woman looking for a good time that I can easily part ways with after one night or a couple.

She's a part of my life, and through Jay, of my job.

Which is why the last few days with her brother have been guilting the hell out of me.

I know what I should do: shut this down, tell her I can't go with her, find her someone else— someone who doesn't want her like I do.

I'm supposed to be looking out for her but I'm questioning whether I can do that without having my own reasons.

My guys need to trust me, and I need to trust myself.

I click into her social media and scroll through pics. Her laughing with friends. Posing with cute captions.

There's one she reposted with a name visible in the corner that has my fist flexing.

"The hell is that?" Jay asks.

I spin to find my teammate looking over my elbow at the screen.

"It's social media. I can teach you how to use it if you want," Rookie calls.

Jay flips him off. "I mean this picture." The story's changed to a repost of one from the account for her sorority.

The caption reads: *Three days! Can't wait to see everyone this weekend!*

Posted by someone with the handle "Carobear," who must be the Caroline she's competing with.

I press a finger to the screen to freeze the image.

One of the people tagged looks familiar. I click

through to his profile, and the name and face have the hairs on my neck lifting.

Kevin Waitrose.

"No fucking way."

Jay grimaces.

"What's wrong?" Rookie asks as he gets up from his set, wiping a towel over his face.

"An asshole my sister went to school with," Jay says. "They dated a while."

"Too long," I spit.

Rookie cocks his head. "You say that like you know the guy."

Jay and I exchange a look.

"I don't like this," Jay grunts.

"I know. But it's not your decision," I point out.

"You didn't see how hard she took it after everything went down back in school, man. You didn't see that prick trying to talk to her at my mom's fundraiser."

This is news to me.

I close the phone and switch back in under the leg press. "Another set. More weight."

"You've already set a new max today," Rookie says.

"More."

His smile fades when he sees I'm serious. "Your funeral, man."

A few other guys on the team look over.

Halfway through the rep, there's a moment I swear it's going to crush me.

I think of Kevin. Prep school grad. White teeth.

Thought he could get away with anything.

Sweat beads on my forehead, streaking down my skin.

I might be a low-key kind of guy, but there are things I won't stand for.

Every ounce of me goes into lifting the weight, as if it's the only thing between me and his piece-of-shit face.

"Everything chill?" Atlas asks when my set is done.

I rub a towel through my hair. "Yeah."

But I'm not chill.

It's unsettling how not chill I am right now.

I spot Jay near the pull-up bar on his phone with an expression like storm clouds.

"What are you doing?"

"Calling Brooke. I'm going to tell her not to go."

No. She needs this event. Plus, it'll piss her off,

start a fight between her and Jay, and that will distract our captain from the work we need to get done on the court.

I wanted to step back, but now there's no way I'm letting her walk into that alone.

I know what I have to do... even if I really don't want to do it.

I grab the phone out of his hand and hit the "Call End" button.

"The hell?!"

I take a breath. "You don't have to worry about her going because... I'm going with her."

The air evaporate from the room.

Everything reduces down to my friend and teammate's expression as he processes my words.

Confusion.

Disbelief.

Anger.

"You *what*?!"

Fuck.

This is not a conversation I planned on having, especially not today.

The Miles Garrett the league and the media know would play it off, joke that it's something casual.

But that's not true, and I'm not sure I could fake it if I wanted to.

"Let's talk about this outside." I nod to the door, unsure of whether he'll deck me before we get there.

We manage to make it into the hall without any bloodshed.

"Talk," Jay demands.

So I skirt as close to reality as I can.

"She wanted someone to have her back this weekend. She asked me to go with her."

"Why you?"

I measure my words. "I think all this sorority stuff got in her head, and she wanted to take someone she could trust. Plus," I deliberately add, "I know you've been worried."

Jay's nostrils flare. "And that prick Kevin is going."

"Guess so." My abs flex.

He paces halfway down the hall before turning back to me. "And you're sure this is a good idea?"

"I've got it under control." I flash teeth in what I hope is a reassuring smile.

He rubs a hand across his hair. "And this is just a favor. You're not hitting on my sister."

The lunch I had an hour ago is suddenly giving me heartburn. "I'm not hitting on your sister."

Jay exhales, nodding.

"Don't do anything stupid. We're not kids, we're the fucking defending champions. And we need you."

BROOKE

Jay: Were you planning on telling me Miles is going to this reunion with you?

"That's it. Men are impossible."

I'm trying to convince myself more than Sierra, and it must not be working because she hands me a shot of tequila with a skeptical look.

It burns all the way down.

I'm mostly pissed that Miles told my brother he's taking me to the reunion after he swore he wouldn't.

I bet he didn't tell my brother we kissed.

Fricking hypocrisy.

I'm on my social and I jump over to Miles's profile.

The last few posts are pics of him sweating and intent on the court. A promo spot with a sports drink. One of him with my brother on the plane, Jay's arm around Miles's shoulders.

"What is it with guys and their little guy clubs?" I mutter to Sierra. "Like they have each other's backs to a fault."

Sierra looks at me, a sympathetic expression on her face. "It's kind of sweet when they do."

"Not when it means they betray your trust." The one thing I asked him to do was keep this a secret for a few weeks. He couldn't even do that.

I'm angry, but more than that, I'm hurt.

Because deep down, it means I wasn't worth keeping a secret for. And no amount of fixed Louboutins or sexy photo shoots can change the truth.

I reach for my phone and hit Miles's contact on impulse.

"It's me," I say when voicemail picks up on the third ring. "I don't need a date. I don't need you pretending to have my back or acting like you care and then spilling my business to your teammates. As of now, my problems are no longer any of your business. And if you're worried I'm obsessing over some dumb kiss that wasn't even any good"— That's a lie, but I'm on a roll, fueled by righteous indignation—"I'm over it."

I finish my drink, say goodbye to Sierra, grab my coat and head for the door.

I'm a dozen furious steps outside when I hear someone shout my name.

"Brooke Ellis! Is that you?"

I turn to find a familiar woman standing with a handsome guy.

"Hannah!" I exclaim.

We hug in greeting, her shiny hair brushing my cheek as I pull away.

"I haven't heard from you in a few months. What are you doing here?" I demand.

"We just moved to Denver for Matt's work." She introduces her husband.

"Classmate from law school?" he guesses.

"Definitely not," I say.

"Brooke and I were sisters," she explains.

But Matt's question reminds me of one of my own. "Did you leave your firm to come here?"

"I did." She sighs. "I might find something in a

year or two, but we just had a baby and I'm enjoying being a mom."

"That's amazing," I say and mean it. "Congratulations."

"Thanks. This is actually our first time leaving her with a sitter for an entire day." Hannah's brows knit with worry.

"She'll be fine," Matt assures her.

We catch up for a few minutes. I wrap my coat tighter around me against the cold.

"Are you excited for this weekend?" Hannah asks. "You're bringing a basketball player, right?"

I blink, thinking of the voicemail I left calling it off.

Hannah is one of the few sisters who was genuinely close with me and Caroline.

"Umm..."

"Isn't that him now?" she asks.

I follow her gaze.

Miles is dressed in a wool coat over gray sweatpants, no hat, color rising up cheeks covered with stubble. He's waving goodbye to a group of fans on the corner, half a head above the tallest of them.

Does he look like he's listened to my voice message?

I'm about to find out, because he's headed this way.

A car passes, and Miles glances down the street before crossing with his hands in his pockets, head down, hair ruffling in the wind as he reaches us.

"Hey."

"Hey," I respond, breathless.

I haven't seen him since his road trip, and he looks good with scruff on his face. His cheek bones are sharper, his eyes brighter.

"This is Hannah. One of my sorority sisters," I emphasize.

"How's it going." He offers a nod to both of them.

His expression betrays nothing.

"We need to get on the same page."

My heart accelerates. *Did he listen to his voicemail?*

If so, this entire plan is about to go sideways. Hannah will find out Miles isn't going to be my date and everyone will think I made it up.

I cut a desperate look toward Hannah and Matt. Whatever she witnesses is going to spread through the reunion in a hot second. I'll be humiliated before I even pick up my name tag at registration, and my future is already on the line.

"I have your back, Brooke Ellis. That hasn't changed." He closes the distance between us. "Your problems are absolutely my business. If you got the sense I don't care about you, then you need to get your eyes checked, Princess."

Miles's cold, bare fingers latch onto my neck.

"What are you doing?" I demand.

"Giving you something new to get worked up about," he murmurs.

I'm dragged upward by the force as his mouth crushes down on mine.

He kisses me as though he's proving a point either to me or both of us.

As though he's tired of being the good guy.

The air is crisp and cool, but his lips are hot and silky. He smells like fresh leaves, and desire curls low in my stomach.

Heat and craving and desperation twine together in my chest, warming me against the cold.

My hands fist in the soft wool of his coat.

I'm lost in how much it feels like he wants this, in how much I do.

When he finally releases me, my heart is galloping at breakneck speed, my knuckles white where they clutch his jacket.

Miles pulls back another inch. His lashes are dark spikes fluttering across my cheeks.

Hannah clears her throat. "Careful next weekend. The resort is built from logs. You two might burn the place down." With a quick admiring smile, she grabs her husband's hand and hurries in the other direction.

18

BROOKE

"*O*MG! Is it really you?!"

"I haven't seen you since Easthampton."

"No, it was Tahoe. Since when are you a brunette?!"

Two women run toward one another across the road to embrace, dodging suitcases and foot traffic.

There's nothing like a massive group of women descending on a mountain tourist town.

The streets are lined with small shops and markets with everything from skiing gear to T-shirts to après-ski outfits. Food vendors and restaurants accommodate the incoming tourists.

Patrons buzz excitedly, the chimes tinkle on

the door of each store, and a bus engine rumbles as it drops off visitors while we walk from the parking lot to the hotel.

The air tastes like wood smoke and peppermint, making me think of hot chocolate.

I feel Miles's arm wrap around my waist protectively as we make our way through the throng of girls toward the lodge that's sorority HQ for the weekend.

A few women stop me to say hi, and I introduce Miles.

He grins, dazzling them.

"Wow, you're a professional athlete," one of them gushes.

"How tall are you?"

"What's it like to win a world championship?"

I look up at him, willing him silently to be brief.

"Yes." "Very." "Great, thank you." On the drive up, I reminded him to answer in monosyllables.

"How long have you been dating?"

My radar goes up. This is in the yellow-flag zone of questioning.

"It's new," I start, but he weighs in.

"When you know, you know."

I glare.

Overkill.

Selling it, he mouths back.

We took Miles's Range Rover, talked about lots of things.

Not the way he kissed the hell out of me. Or the fact that he outed me to my brother.

That part hasn't come up.

The thing is, our bickering feels good—as good as the attraction between us that has him touching me, holding the door when I get back in the car after a rest stop, teasing me for my taste in music. It distracts me from everything that's on the line this weekend.

"Here is your agenda for the day. First up, we have fun activities. Then dinner. Then a special ceremony after," the sister running orientation explains as we reach the front of the line.

I browse the agenda as we switch to the check-in line for our rooms.

Miles peers over my shoulder. "You forgot to buy me pink outfits."

When we reach the front desk, I give them my name.

"We have you in a queen room," the agent says, taking my credit card.

I blink. "I asked for two queens."

Someone else is trying to talk to my date, and he's not listening to my conversation. We're surrounded by people, and it feels suspicious to argue when Miles is supposed to be my boyfriend.

The desk agent furrows her brows, tapping at her keyboard. "I don't see that in our system." Another minute ticks by, and she shakes her head. "We could ask another guest if they'll switch?"

And let them know Miles and I aren't really together? No way.

"It's fine. Great." I smile and pluck the key card from her hand.

When I pictured all the things we'd be doing together to bolster my confidence and chances of winning this deal, I didn't imagine spending two nights lying next to him.

The man I've gotten off to.

The same one who might be better at kissing than at basketball.

But I can't afford to get distracted.

My rent is due soon, and my bank account is next-level empty.

Maybe there will be a couch.

The rooms are situated in a bunch of small, cabin-like structures dotting the resort property and linked by gravel paths.

As we take our stuff to the room, I tell Miles, "You look good carrying bags. You do this for all your girlfriends?"

"It's been a minute since I called someone my girl. And I haven't introduced a woman to my Grams before."

I let his words sink in as he adjusts the duffel on his back.

"I meant what I said. I care and it's not an act."

Gravel crunches under our feet. I focus on that as he goes on.

"I didn't say anything about your financial situation and the only reason I told Jay I agreed to come was that he was worried about you and Kevin. I told him I was going to look out for you."

"Is that what you're going to do?" I risk a glance over at him.

The beat before he answers is only slightly longer than necessary.

"Yeah."

We get to the cabin designated on our paperwork and find the room. Ours is one of six sharing a building.

I reach for my key and swipe it next to the handle.

The door of the room swings wide. The planks in the floor creak as I walk inside.

The room is big with a fireplace and a fur—probably faux fur—rug.

There's no couch.

And the bed...

I feel Miles's eyes on me as I set my bag on the stand and glance around the room.

"It's not two queens." I state the obvious.

"That's not even one."

He's not wrong. The lone double bed stares up at us, the cozy navy duvet doing nothing to mask the postage stamp of mattress.

"We can share the bed." I take my weekender bag from him and drop it on the bed.

Better than me being responsible for an NBA player messing up his back.

"Which side do you sleep on?" I ask.

"I don't."

The image of him taking up the entire bed, his body sprawled across the sheets, enters without permission.

"How do you sleep next to another human?"

"I don't."

"Never?" I prompt. "You've never let a woman stay over? Never crashed in another human's bed?"

He cocks his head. "There was a pileup after the all-star game, but no one remembers that."

My lips curve as I work on the zipper of my bag. I manage to get it open and start unpacking, starting with my pajamas.

"You could've kept him from finding out if you wanted to." I say it without turning.

"But if I was him and I found out my loyal teammate didn't mention he was taking my sister out, I'd be asking why the hell not."

I'm not sure what to say to that.

I manage to avoid Caroline exactly as long as it takes to get to our first activity.

"Brooke! So amazing to see you in person. It's been too long." We swap cheek kisses.

"Everything looks beautiful," I say sincerely.

"Well, it's important to have these events," she says, just as earnest. Her attention shifts to the man at my side. "Miles, wonderful to see you again also," she adds as he holds out a hand.

"Again?" he prompts.

Her smile tightens. "We've met before. Back in college."

"Have we?" he asks, looking confused.

I could hug him.

"We'll catch up at dinner," Caroline promises.

She turns and disappears into the crowd. There are a few hundred sisters and their dates, and I deliberately did not seat us at the same table, but there's no time to think about it.

The day is filled with team-building activities and games, some of which are actual fun. We were instructed to dress in activewear, so for the afternoon, I'm in leggings and Miles is in shorts.

Our first activity is a scavenger hunt. Miles and I work well together, and we quickly gain the upper hand over the other teams.

I can't help but feel conscious of Miles's presence. Every time our eyes meet, I feel a jolt of electricity pass between us as we run through the streets, collecting clues and solving riddles.

When we're done, I spot Elise surrounded by a group of women.

"Elise!" I cut through the crowd of Kappas and partners to the stunning woman with a chic brunette bob and a knit two-piece set. She's giving Audrey Hepburn vibes, glamorous but somehow attainable.

"Brooke, lovely to see you. And Miles Garrett!"

She introduces her husband, who starts talking to Miles.

"My husband is a big Kodiaks fan," she confides in me.

I do an imaginary fist pump.

"Well, don't rush off. There's time before dinner to catch up."

Miles looks between us. "Let's let the ladies catch up. Why don't we play a little three-on-three?"

Her husband's eyes widen with delight.

"You're on your day off," Elise says, giving him an out.

"It's my pleasure," he says smoothly.

God, I could kiss him.

"Go easy on them," I call as Miles and the husband gather another four guys to their cause, which takes all of thirty seconds.

A crowd gathers before someone finds a basketball.

He lifts his shirt to wipe his face and my throat dries.

"What did you want to talk about?" Elise asks.

I force myself to concentrate. The stakes are too high to screw up.

"I'm a huge fan of your company, and excited

for the new line you're announcing. It's going to be a game changer. Can you tell me more about your distribution?"

Elise happily complies. "We're seeking one person to really be the public face of the campaign. We've had several influencers approach us on this, actually, and we want to get this right."

"I'd love to be considered."

"The schedule this weekend is pretty packed, but let's find a time to talk more."

When I finish with Elise, Miles jogs over. "How'd it go?"

"I think she's open but I didn't get a commitment yet."

Miles nods. "I signed some stuff for him and offered to show him around when he's in Denver."

My heart flips over in my chest. "I guess we make a pretty good team."

"Guess we do, Princess."

He hooks an arm around my shoulders, and we head back side by side.

"Little Sis!" Ruby hollers.

I run across the dining room and throw myself into her arms. "It's so good to see you."

"Sorry I'm late. Emergency."

"You missed scavenger hunts and pin-swap ceremonies, but you'll hear about every minute because you're sitting at our table."

Miles and I take our seats, close enough together that our legs brush underneath the table.

We took turns showering after the afternoon's activities, me trying not to think about how hot he looked playing basketball with the other guys.

Now I'm wearing a cute minidress and chestnut-brown heels that make my legs look extra long. He's in chinos and a button-down shirt and looks like Hamptons sailboat porn. I'm congratulating and cursing myself for taking an already smoking-hot professional athlete and making him sinfully sexy.

"You must be Miles," Ruby says, extending a hand. "I'm Ruby, Brooke's big sis from school."

"Doctor, right? She talks about you a lot." Miles smiles easily, and Ruby's eyes brighten with delight.

"I'm glad she talked about that and not the pranks we pulled."

"Oh yeah? Let's hear it."

They swap stories, and I bite my cheek as I listen to them. I didn't expect Miles and Ruby to hit it off, but his easygoing vibe and her professional veneer work together. I'm actually having a good time until Caroline sits on her other side... with my ex.

Seeing Kevin right across the table is worse than seeing him at my mom's event. At least there, I could sprint the other way.

You put them here? Ruby mouths.

I shake my head and glance at the table cards. Someone moved them around.

I'm willing to bet that someone was Caroline.

"Small world," Kevin says.

His attention flicks to Miles, his smile faltering, replaced by coolness.

It used to take a lot for Kevin to be intimidated. It feels good that Miles sets him on edge.

"I thought Hannah was sitting here," I say with a smile. I'd put her and Matt at our table after we ran into them, remembering how much I enjoyed her.

Caroline waves a hand. "She's not coming. It's better this way."

I frown. "Better how? You were inseparable."

"You're obviously misremembering. She never had her priorities in order. I don't know why we accepted her into Kappa in the first place."

I pull out my phone and find Hannah's contact and send off a quick message.

When I tuck the phone away, Kevin is flirting shamelessly with Caroline. He plays with a piece of her hair, grinning at her.

We're long over, but it still messes with my insecurities that she's better than me in some way I can't fix.

Out of nowhere, Miles's hand brushes against mine under the table. I glance over, and he gives me a reassuring smile. It's as if he knows what I'm thinking, knows how I'm feeling. I'm grateful for him yet again.

"Brooke, you must be happy to find a guy taller than you," Caroline starts. "You were always so statuesque."

"It is a relief," I say, playing along.

One of the other girls at our table leans in. "I bet he barely fits in your bed."

Without missing a beat, Miles presses a kiss to my forehead. "We don't need a bed, do we, Princess?"

I'm too surprised to respond, but Ruby laughs

into her drink. Caroline's eyes narrow so dramatically she could be asleep if it wasn't for the tight lines around her lips.

The lights are dimmed, and a hush falls over the room.

My phone buzzes with a message. I discreetly check it to find a response.

Hannah: Hey! Thanks for checking in. I felt so bad for canceling, but the baby's been sick the last two days. I said I might be able to come for the second day, but Caroline said it would mess up the numbers. Have the best time!

I tuck the phone back into my bag, staring at Caroline's profile in the dark.

"Welcome to the Kappa reunion," a voice booms through the speakers. "Tonight, we celebrate sisterhood, friendship, and love. Now, I'd like to welcome our alumni chapter president to say a few words."

Elise goes up to the microphone to warm applause.

"College is a time when we strike out on our own, leaving our parents and siblings behind as we forge new identities for ourselves. It's when we form new connections. It's when we choose our families."

My chest tightens. I didn't expect to get emotional over a single speech.

"Sisterhood is about having each other's backs, living the ups and downs of life, accepting who we want to be but also who we are right now."

She continues for another few minutes, ending to even more applause than when she started.

Dinner is served, and we make small talk between courses and speakers.

Shortly before dessert, I watch Caroline walk over to the head table where Elise is sitting with our other uber-successful alum—I considered seating her with us, but it felt like an overt abuse of power—and say something to her.

The woman looks surprised, but rises and follows Caroline out of the room.

"Where are they off to?" I whisper to Miles.

He shakes his head.

I stand, smoothing my dress. "Excuse me," I say and slip out after the two women.

When I reach the hallway, there's no sign of them.

Warning bells go off in my mind.

Caroline knows I'm pitching Elise. She's trying to get in first.

Not happening.

I stalk down the hallways like a hunter in search of prey.

I've walked nearly an entire square of the facility and stuck my head outside without spotting them.

Finally, I spot a door labeled "PRIVATE" with a sign taped over it that reads "STAFF ONLY."

I push inside.

The room is a large office with half a dozen empty desks in open-concept style. A pinboard on the wall has upcoming events being held at the venue. There's another closed door near the entry.

I step toward it, turning the handle cautiously as I push it inward.

Darkness. Inside is some kind of closet. Coats, maybe, or supplies. I feel the inside for a lightswitch—

"What are you doing?"

The male voice has me spinning.

It's Miles, standing in the open doorway to the hall.

Relief has my shoulders sagging.

I tug him in and shut the door.

"I thought Caroline went in here," I whisper loudly. "I need to find her and Elise."

"And you figured they'd be updating spreadsheets in their cocktail dresses?" He glances around.

"This is Caroline we're talking about. I'm not going to let her pull one over on me again."

I shoot him a look, distracted again by how gorgeous he is in the clothes I picked out. "You clean up really well, you know that?"

His lips tip up. "Thought you weren't indulging my ego."

I try to resist smiling, but I can't help it. "Just this once."

Voices sound outside.

"Shit! We're going to get caught," I gasp.

Normally, I can think on my feet, but suddenly my heels are glued to the carpet, my body paralyzed.

The handle turns.

Miles steps close to me. The expression on his

face has my nerves dancing as much as the prospect of getting caught.

"Play along, Princess."

He grabs my hand.

The last thought I have is how delicious his skin feels on mine before he drags me into the closet.

19

BROOKE

*W*e're seconds from being busted, but you wouldn't know it from the way Miles spins me to face him.

My back hits a rack of coats. He steps between my thighs, his hand skimming up my skin under my dress as his mouth descends to my throat.

His teeth.

Dear God, there's no better feeling than this man's teeth on my skin.

Unless it's his tongue. Or his lips.

I'm unprepared for all of it, and the sensations rip a moan from me.

Everything feels so damn *good*.

My fingers stretch up his shirt to lace behind his neck.

Voices enter my brain. I start to pull back, but Miles grabs me closer.

He tugs up my dress, hitching my leg around his, squeezing my thigh.

With a swift movement, Miles lifts me and pins me against the wall of the coat closet. My legs wrap around his waist. His hard length pressing against me sends a surge of desire through every nerve ending in my body.

"Brooke," he groans into my skin.

Conversation is happening outside, urgent voices, but they're a distant blur.

What he's doing to me in here is far more important.

He grabs my ass, grinding into me.

My breath catches. My fingers dig into his shoulders, the muscles there.

The scent of him fills my senses, intoxicating and arousing.

The confined space of the coat closet amplifies every moan and whimper that escapes our lips, heightening the intensity.

I bite my lip, fighting back another moan as he nibbles on my earlobe before trailing kisses down the nape of my neck.

His fingers inch toward the apex of my thighs.

Desire floods me. Each stroke sends electric shivers down my spine, igniting a fire within me that threatens to consume us both.

The door swings wide. "What the...?"

I force my eyes open.

Caroline's behind with another couple members of the executive of the sorority.

"What are you doing in here?"

"Thought that was obvious." Miles' smile is cocky, his hair deliciously disheveled from my fingers. "This dress has been fucking with my head all night."

We stay pressed against each other, our ragged breaths mingling in the small space.

Caroline composes herself. "It's almost time."

Most of the weekend is more practical—networking, fundraising, some unstructured social time—but the hour inside the hall at the resort is about remembering our Kappa sisters and the bonds we've shared.

Dates aren't permitted in this part of the agenda. Miles said he was going to explore or possibly hit the gym.

Each of us is given a candle as we filter into the room.

(Flameless, as Caroline lamented a few weeks ago in an email to the organizing committee, but necessary for insurance purposes given the resort is a log structure.)

When I take a seat next to Ruby and a handful of other women from our class, I feel a hit of shame over the way I chased Caroline and Elise out of dinner.

There probably wasn't any secret plot and it is rejuvenating to see friends I haven't spent time with in months or years. The summer after junior year, things were tense enough I didn't enjoy myself.

Maybe I missed out.

Caroline speaks from the front, leading the room in reciting the Kappa pledge.

When we're finished, she takes a moment to recognize specific sisters for their contributions. It really is impressive.

"As president of our class," she concludes, "I'm proud to say that each sister from our entire executive is here, and—"

"Not everyone," I murmur to Ruby.

"What was that?" Caroline leans over the podium.

A hundred heads swivel to where I'm seated in the third row.

"Hannah isn't here," I go on at the questioning looks.

Caroline's smile tightens. "Well..." She's clearly annoyed at being interrupted. "That hardly counts."

"Why not? She's just as much a Kappa as anyone. Just because she's taking care of her family instead of being a partner or an entrepreneur or..." I search for the words. "... some hotshot doctor." I turn to Ruby.

"No offence," I whisper.

"None taken."

Caroline grips the podium, resetting her smile. "Kappas are breaking glass ceilings everywhere," she informs me. "Protecting women's rights to be high achievers."

"What about women's rights to do whatever they want? I thought the point was allowing women to choose and not have to pretend."

I look around at the wary and startled faces in the crowd before going on.

"Some of the people in this room and

generations of women before them say they're creating opportunities for sisters, but what they mean is a certain kind of opportunity.

"We don't like to talk about people who don't fit the mold. We're all way too obsessed with how things look."

Scanning the audience again, this time I find a few grudging nods.

It wasn't my intention to start something, but it seems I'm not the only one who feels this way.

When my gaze returns to the front, Caroline's stiff and icy. "Perhaps you should have been more concerned with how things looked when you were this close to getting the entire Kappa house shut down over your substance abuse problem, Brooke Ellis."

A collective gasp goes up.

I feel like I've been slapped.

The room isn't sure what to believe, and Caroline can't tell who's on her side.

I wait for a strategy to rush up at me, but I'm blank as a sheet of paper.

My hand tingles. It's Ruby, clasping my palm in both of hers in support.

I tug my hand away with an apologetic look for my contrite friend and start toward the doors.

On my way, I spot Elise, her face pale and stunned.

There goes my chance to rep her brand.

The realization devastates me, but there's nothing I can do.

Busting through the doors and stalking down the hall, I'm vaguely aware of nearby laughter. Some guys are drinking and playing cards.

"Brooke." Miles's voice comes from somewhere behind me, sounding concerned. "Brooke, wait."

I don't turn to look at him.

The only thing that matters is that I get the hell out of here.

MILES

She's running down the hall. I can barely keep up even with much longer legs.

I catch up to her at the end, where she's leaning against the wall with her head bowed. It's clear that whatever happened in that room hit her hard, and I don't want to make things worse.

"Brooke," I say softly, leaning against the wall next to her. "Tell me what's wrong."

She looks up at me, her eyes wide. "Coming here was a mistake."

I put a hand on her back, rubbing soothing circles.

I feel her trembling slightly, and I wrap my arms around her tightly, holding her close. It feels as if we've been doing this forever, as though we've been together for years instead of a few days.

Brooke takes a deep breath, her hand reaching for mine.

"I can't handle being in that room right now. I'm so angry. But I'm still here because I *need* to make it work. I can be disgusted with them, but I still need Elise. No matter how hard I try to get away from it, at the end of the day, it feels like all anyone cares about is appearances. They believe whatever they want to believe and tell whatever stories suit them."

The wavering in her voice and her words breaks my heart.

"We don't have to go back there," I say, stroking her palm with my thumb.

Brooke nods, squeezing my hand. I don't think she realizes she's doing it.

I lead her back down the hallway until we find

an empty room and sit on the floor inside, leaning against the wall. The silence stretches between us.

"What kind of stories?" I can't help asking.

"Back in junior year before exams, Caroline confronted me saying she found coke in my room. A lot of coke."

"I'm guessing you don't mean the drink."

"I do not." Her laugh is tired. "She reported it to the administration and aggressively tried to get me kicked out. It almost worked, too."

The woman in front of me might be impulsive, but something about the story rings false.

"Everyone makes mistakes," I say slowly. "But what aren't you telling me?"

Her eyes lift to my face, the guilt and shame pouring out of her.

"It wasn't mine."

20

MILES

"It was Kevin's," she says on an exhale. "He said he was keeping it for a friend. I didn't like it. He pressured me, and I told him it was fine even though it wasn't.

"I tried explaining to Caroline that it was a misunderstanding. She claims she didn't turn me in, but there's no one else it could have been. It escalated so fast that my mom had to get involved." Brooke shudders. "She couldn't have a daughter getting charged or expelled or both, so she made a big donation to the administration. A week later, Kevin broke up with me."

Her eyes cloud as though she's reliving it.

"What did your mom say about covering for Kevin?"

She takes a slow breath. "I never told her. His family is a major campaign donor. It would have put her in an even worse spot."

Fuck.

I pretend to be shocked.

The thing is... I'm not.

But I hurt for her like it's fresh.

I get it—why she tries so hard to present herself a certain way, why she doesn't feel like she can let loose even when she wants to.

We sit there for a while longer, holding each other and taking comfort in each other's presence.

"I should go back and face them." She yawns on the last word.

"Do it in the morning."

I rise first and help her up.

As we navigate toward the doors of the main building, Brooke leans into me, her head resting on my shoulder.

Outside, the cold night air hits us in a gust. I wrap my arm around her waist, holding her close.

The only sound is our footsteps on the gravel path as we head for our cabin. The moon is high in the sky, casting a soft light over the trees and cabins. It's a beautiful night, but it's hard to appreciate it when Brooke is hurting.

When we arrive at the cabin, I open the door and let Brooke in first. She heads straight to our shared room, and I follow her, closing the door softly. Brooke sits on the bed.

My phone buzzes and I curse. "Be right back."

She nods, wrapping her arms around herself.

I turn away to look at the screen.

It's Jay.

I don't want to leave Brooke.

Still, Jay is my friend. My team captain. The person I owe my loyalty to.

I duck into the bathroom as a compromise so I don't have to leave the room and pull the door closed.

"Yeah," I answer under my breath.

"How are things going?"

I stare at the phone. Normally, I'm down for a surprise call from one of my teammates, but this isn't the time.

"We're pretty busy here."

"Right. But you'd tell me if something was wrong."

I glance at the closed door. "Of course I would."

I'm conflicted.

"Don't do anything stupid."

"Stupid like what?"

There's silence.

"Back when I first met you, we were all struggling to find our way."

"We were kids," I counter.

"And you've proven yourself. We've all had to in our own ways. But I guess what I'm saying is... we need you, man."

The responsibility feels suffocating.

When I emerge, Brooke's lying still on the bed facing the other way. I brush my teeth in the bathroom and change into cotton pajama pants.

"Brooke?" I ask when I return.

There's no answer.

I drop into a chair opposite the fireplace and stare sightlessly at my phone. A sound reaches my ears.

Shaky breathing.

I drop the phone on the coffee table, my hands fisting.

I promised I'd look out for her from a safe distance.

But listening to her quiet sobs is torture.

Fuck this.

BROOKE

Crying isn't something I do often.

Sadness means sorrow, regret.

I don't let myself regret.

The bed creaks behind me, the mattress dipping as Miles shifts in behind me.

His warm chest heats my shoulders, and I stiffen. "What are you...?"

His arm wraps around me, pulls me back against him.

Gentle.

Insistent.

"Don't," I whisper.

"Don't what?" His voice is low and soothing, a rumble against my shoulder. "Don't hold you when it's damned obvious that's what you need?"

I try to fight him. The careful effort I put into my appearance is long gone, replaced by a makeup-stained face and a T-shirt I pulled on after ripping off the dress I chose for dinner.

He doesn't let go. He reaches for the hair stuck to my face and smooths it behind my ear.

I cry for real. Miles holds me tighter, his hand rubbing soothing circles on my back. I feel safe and comforted in his embrace, knowing that he won't judge me for my tears.

I let out all my frustration, my pain, my anger, and my sadness. I cry until there are no more tears left, until my sobs turn into soft whimpers, until I'm completely drained.

Years of feeling as if I have to prove myself worthy every single day, of defending the things I want to be proud of.

Eventually, Miles disappears into the bathroom and returns moments later with a glass of water.

I take a long drink. He's a silhouette as he retrieves the glass from me and sets it on the nightstand.

"You probably think I'm a mess," I manage.

"I think you're beautiful."

Miles shifts back onto the bed, and I feel his body heat against mine again. It's comforting.

"Growing up, my mom used to tell us, 'It's what they see that matters,'" I say. "She said she meant that we should always do our best, but I took it as meaning you should protect your image at all costs. I went to the best schools, made the right friends, wore the right clothes, dated the right boys."

I think of Kevin.

"But at a certain point, I realized how much of it was an act. The smiling pictures. The surface-level acceptance. And the truth is, some people get away with behaving badly. They get a hundred chances."

"I'm going to say something I have no business saying." Miles's breath warms my neck. "I'm glad he dumped you."

I chuckle, my throat thick. "Because it means you got to come to this amazing weekend as my fake boyfriend years later?"

"Because there is no universe in which a prick like that deserves to be with a woman like you."

His words don't only smooth over my rough surfaces, they heal them.

I take a shaky breath.

Tomorrow, I need to decide what to do—about the contract, about the sorority, all of it.

But not tonight.

"Why did you do it?" I ask, my voice barely above a whisper.

He shifts. "Do what?"

"Come to this reunion with me."

His hand traces slow circles on my back, one

after another. "You needed someone. I wanted to be that person."

I turn my head to look at him. My chest aches.

Miles watches me for a moment, his eyes searching mine in the dark. "You deserve to have someone in your corner. Not because you're smart or beautiful or kind, although you are all of those things. Because you were born worthwhile, and nothing you or anyone else does or says can change that."

That kind of caring can be just as easily reversed, a voice reminds me. Kevin dropped me with zero warning after years together, even after I covered for his fuck-up. My mom decided to end her ongoing investment in me based on a single photo.

But I feel a flicker of hope that it's possible for someone to care about me for who I am.

So, tonight I let myself believe.

21

MILES

It's strange how waking up with another person feels so...

Personal.

The light shafting through the window behind me dances across her parted lips.

You notice details you never thought you would. Like how soft her skin is—softer than the silk pillowcase under her head—where my thumbs brush her sides under her sleep shirt.

At some point, my leg got threaded between hers, or she wound hers around mine.

Her dark lashes twitch against her cheeks as she dreams.

Her full lips part.

I want to lean in, slide my tongue between

them like I would've done if we'd had ten more seconds in the closet before getting busted.

Last night was about comfort. I wanted to be there for her when she was going through a shitty time.

This morning, our bodies twined together under the sheets, the scent of her filling my nostrils...

Nothing about this is comforting.

I study her face, taking in every detail: the curve of her nose, the arch of her eyebrows, the way her hair falls across her forehead.

The room is quiet except for the sound of our breathing and the faint rustle of the sheets as we shift. When she sighs, a little puff of contentedness, my hand itches. The only way to relieve it is to move, tracing the curve of her waist, the gentle slope of her hip.

I hear a sound from outside, a door slamming.

Her body shifts slightly, but her breathing remains even, and her grip on me only tightens.

Now she's pressing herself against my thigh as if it's the most natural thing in the world.

I'm already hard, because hello, morning. But even if I wasn't, I would be from her closeness, from the way she smells.

My body throbs with the insistence that I have to have her.

I know that I could. Right now, she wouldn't refuse me.

I could coax her onto her back, tease her awake with my lips on her throat, the curve of her breast. Slide my hand between her soft thighs, playing, until she's arching against me.

Tease her until she's begging me to sink inside her the way we've both been pretending we don't need.

But last night, she was hurting and vulnerable. I don't want to take advantage of her.

Plus, I'd be abusing Jay's trust in a way there's no coming back from.

Everything up to last night, including the closet groping, is defensible, at least in part. Ends justify the means and all that.

I can't think of what I'd say to him if I did the things to his sister that I want to right now.

In the end, it's the guilt that makes me ease out of bed, careful not to wake her.

In the shower, I dunk my head under the stream of hot water and wait for my muscles to ease.

My eyes squeeze shut, and suddenly I'm picturing her skin, her lips, the feel of her.

My cock is somehow harder than it was a second ago.

The knot in my shoulders refuses to budge.

I wrap my fingers around my length and grip tight.

I need to get through today. To be there for her. To protect her the way I promised Jay I would.

To do that, I have to get rid of this feeling.

I stroke my length and hiss between my tight jaw. I can't even say it feels good. It feels *necessary*, as though there's no way I can breathe or talk or walk without relieving the ache that comes from being around her.

My knuckles turn white against the tile. My ass clenches as I fuck my own hand, wishing it was the girl in the other room.

I want those dark eyes on mine, glazed with desire as she falls over the edge with my name on her lips, forgetting every asshole she's ever met.

My come blends with the water, slipping down the drain and leaving no trace of my guilt.

When I get out, she's still asleep. I get dressed and leave a note by the door in case she wakes up while I'm out. I go for a walk to the dining room.

On the way, I check my phone.

There's a message from the team with an update about practice tomorrow. A note from my dog sitter with a video of Waffles in which he's being asked to say 'hi to Daddy.' Waffles, for his part, munches happily on a treat like he doesn't care if I'm alive or dead.

I send a text to Grams to check in. There's no immediate response, but that's not strange.

In the dining room, there's coffee and breakfast. A range of mostly unfamiliar faces. A few people wave to me and make small talk—the risk of being something of a celebrity.

"Miles." Brooke's friend from last night smiles in greeting and gestures me over.

"Hey, Ruby. Looks like you've been up a minute." I nod to her lap, the stack of papers and notes there, and her phone sitting on top.

"No rest for an ER doc. Brooke still asleep?" she asks, a half smile on her face.

I nod.

"What she did last night was brave. Rocking the boat is dangerous."

"I've always liked that about her."

"Me too." Ruby tilts her head, eyes narrowing

thoughtfully. "She needs someone in her corner. You up for the challenge, Mr. NBA Champion?"

The answer hits me without hesitation.

Yeah, I am.

An idea comes together. How I can be there for Brooke today, show her how amazing she is.

Ruby's phone jumps in her lap. "Shit."

"You need another hand. Can I get you a coffee?"

"With cream. Thanks." She smiles and hits Answer. "Dr. Robinson."

After getting Ruby's coffee, I'm packing up breakfast to go, plus coffees for Brooke and me, when I run into a familiar face.

"What are you doing here?" Kevin demands.

I straighten as I finish pouring the first coffee. "Thought we went over this last night. I'm here with Brooke." I reach for the second cup.

He shakes his head. "You were always too close. Why were you hanging around a college campus when you got drafted?"

"New team didn't have the Doritos flavors they did in the dining hall on campus."

"Right. That's what kept you coming back."

My molars grind softly. There are at least a

dozen people around. *Be smart*, a voice says in my head. *Jay's voice.*

I finish getting our coffees from the drip machine. Been gone a day and I miss the hell out of my espresso.

"My face healed better than ever, thanks for asking."

I turn to find Kevin goading me from the other side of the breakfast area. A few people look over and I ignore them.

I stack the coffees in one hand and cross to him.

"Kevin. My dude." I flash teeth as I clap a friendly-looking hand on his shoulder. "You're going to stay far away from Brooke. Here. Back in Denver." The way we're standing, it probably looks as if I'm confiding the latest basketball gossip, or reminding him of an inside joke. "You don't get a second of her time and attention. If I'd been around back when she decided to let you be her sorry ass excuse for a boyfriend, you wouldn't have gotten it then, either. You understand?"

I have the satisfaction of watching his eyes widen before he can control his reaction.

"It's not college anymore, and you can't touch me," he calls after me as I head for the door, careful not to crush the coffee cup in my fist.

22

BROOKE

There's a reason I don't cry.

It's not fun or sexy. It's not a good time before, during, or after.

I roll to my back, stretching out with long, languid movements. My eyes feel as if I rubbed them with sandpaper. My chest aches hollowly.

Except...

Maybe I was wrong because I also feel as if a huge weight has been lifted away and I can breathe.

I fell asleep in Miles's arms.

The sheets smell like him, and I inhale the scent of him on the pillow.

I leaned on him last night. More than I'd

planned. More than my pride would ordinarily let me.

The sky didn't fall.

Maybe there's something to letting another person in.

My phone buzzes. There's a message from my landlord reminding me that my rent was due yesterday.

I click off, dropping the phone and falling back against the wooden headboard.

I need to land this contract. Otherwise, I'll be out a place to live, not to mention groceries.

The door latch sounds, and I bolt upright.

"Hi," Miles says as he enters, balancing two cardboard cups on top of one another in his right hand, the key in his left.

"Hey." My voice is thick with sleep, and I clear my throat. "How's the coffee?"

"Not as good as mine."

I smile and he passes over one cup.

Miles looks good. He always looks good, but he's showered and his hair is damp. His dark jeans cling to strong legs, his sweater a moodier version of the blue of his eyes.

"What time is it?" I ask.

"Nine."

"Shit." I straighten immediately. "We need to be at breakfast. I need to reassure everyone I haven't lost my mind, starting with Elise." I shift out of bed, pulling a robe over my sleep shirt. "And explain why she should give me the contract instead of Caroline, and do it before we leave tomorrow, and..."

Miles shifts in front of me, blocking my way. "Or you can take a shower and we can have breakfast to go." He holds up a paper bag.

I'm instantly suspicious. "To go where?"

His eyes dance as he grins. "You wanted to disappear last night. So disappear with me, Princess."

"You're insane!" I shriek over the wind as my heart hammers. The hot air balloon is a staggering work of purple fabric and fire, lifting us higher with every second.

After I spilled out of bed and savored the hot breakfast and hotter shower, Miles drove us just out of town and parked next to a field where a massive purple hot air balloon was inflating.

"We're going up in that?" I demanded.

"The crew here is the best. They're in charge of all the festivals and events in the area. Don't worry."

I wasn't worried.

I was excited.

Now, we're hundreds of feet in the air and my problems feel as far away as the receding ground. I lean over the edge of the hot air balloon to take in the scenery, and Miles grabs my arm.

"Afraid I'm going to jump?" I taunt over my shoulder.

"Nah. Just don't want you to fall."

His lips are close to my ear, and his body presses against mine. The proximity affects me as always, only up here it's possible the altitude adds to the effect.

Behind us, the operator minds his own business. The balloon basket holds up to ten guests, but today, it's a private flight for two. He gave us safety instructions earlier and is leaving us to ourselves. I'm guessing this is a common date activity, and I can see why.

Miles is handsome as hell. When I glance back at him, his hoodie is plastered to his hard body from the wind, his dark hair whipping around his head. He squints into the sun, surveying the view with genuine appreciation and delight.

Except he's not looking at the scenery.

He's looking at me.

"We never finished those date questions," I tell him, and he grins.

"Let's go, then."

"My biggest fear..." I take a breath. "Is that the entire world will find out I'm not who I pretend to be. That I'm not capable or polished or organized. That even though my family did everything to give me a bright future, invested in me every step of the way, I managed to fuck it up." I cut a look at him. "You?"

"Having to choose between things I love."

I lean my head against his bicep. "It's a good problem to have. If the choice is a hard one, it means you have a life worth living."

Somewhere during appreciating how small we are up here, how much we don't matter, I realize the truth: I'm going to be all right.

No matter the balance of my bank account or my future prospects, Miles makes me feel as though my world is in order.

The wind carries away the sound of the engine

as it gushes over our heads. Beneath the basket, acres and acres of fields drift under us. The town of Vail. Even the lodge is tiny and insignificant.

Miles points toward the ground, pulling me close so his lips brush my ear. "There's our cabin."

"There's Caroline." I smudge a finger over her head. "Kidding. I won't murder her. Or Kevin."

It's a joke, but Miles stiffens behind me. "It's better if you stay away from him."

"I was planning on it," I say lightly.

The basket bounces on an air current, and Miles's arms tighten around me.

"Last night, I was so angry," I tell him. "I overreacted. But Miles... I wanted to see the whole place up in flames."

"Maybe you need to burn some things down and start over."

I lean back against his chest. "You're a team player." His chuckle rumbles through my back. "How do you do it? Especially when you don't want to?"

He lifts a piece of my hair between his fingers, tugging lightly. "You remember why it matters."

I twist in his arms, just enough to make eye contact. "I'm going to see Elise when we get back,"

I decide. "See if she'll meet me this afternoon. I'll explain what happened and make her see this is the right fit."

The flash of approval on his face lights me up. "That's my girl."

23

BROOKE

I stake out the main lodge until I see Elise emerge from the spa.

"There you are!" I descend on her with a broad smile. "I hope you had a wonderful massage."

"How did you know I'd be here?"

"Luck, I guess."

That, and Miles flirting with the spa assistant so I could sneak a look at their appointment list for the day.

"I was hoping we'd get time to talk. I wanted to explain what happened last night at the ceremony."

Her brows lift. "It was certainly... unexpected."

"I know. But I needed to make sure that all our sisters were mentioned."

"Why?" she asks.

"It matters. I believe that we should champion one another, help every sister become who she wants to be in the world. And part of that is not putting judgment on her."

She turns over my words. "You display a lot of leadership qualities, and I know from building my business that it takes more than a yes-woman to get things done."

Elise reaches into her bag for a cream cashmere sweater and tugs it over her head. "But you're not the only strong candidate," she says, straightening the sleeves.

"I'm sure. But I think I can do the best job. For instance." I nod to the sweater she pulled on. "Is that from your new collection?"

"It is."

"So, I love the inset sleeve." I point to the seam, my finger brushing the wool. "The crew neck is classic, but the sleeve makes it more modern. It's obviously grade-A cashmere from the softness, the knit, and the fact you pulled it out of your bag and it drapes that well."

Her lips twitch at the corners. "Is that all?"

"No. A lot of people look at clothing and think it's either utilitarian or frivolous, but a great outfit is an experience. It's who you are mixed with how you want to show up. If you're down, a cozy sweater can lift you higher. If you're afraid, a bold jacket can lend you confidence. In other words... it's one thing to wear clothes, and it's another to know why you're doing it."

Elise reaches into her bag for sunglasses, her lips curving. "I'm in alumni chapter events for the rest of the afternoon but will make my decision soon. There's a big launch of winter clothes happening shortly, and we need to coordinate with our influencers."

My heart leaps.

I catch up with Miles around the corner of the building, still giddy with anticipation.

"How'd it go?" he asks.

"She's going to have her office call me after the weekend."

He drags me into his arms for a hug.

Nothing feels as good as his strong arms around me.

I did this. We did this. It wouldn't have happened without him.

The weekend is almost over, but I don't want it to be.

Here, he's mine.

Even if it's all a game.

A sister goes running by with pink flyers. *Midnight hot tubs.* Half a dozen are located around the resort.

"Huh. There's one near us," Miles observes.

"We should do it."

He rubs a hand over his jaw, his expression impossible to read.

"Am I that difficult?" I murmur it as if the answer won't hurt.

"No," he says, drawing out the word. "When we're together, it's easy, Brooke. It's so fucking easy with you."

His eyes are a thousand feet deep. I could drown in them.

Suddenly, I want everything he'll give me. Even if it's selfish. Even if it's temporary.

"What do you say? One more night of pretending?" My throat is dry.

Miles lowers his face, his nose bumping mine. "Like a victory lap."

I nod. I'm desperate to arch toward him, my fingers digging into his arms.

The hot tub promoter runs past the doors of the spa. "Let's go, everyone! One night of partying! We're a long way from Denver!" she hollers.

She's right, I decide as I look into Miles's intent, handsome face.

We're a long way from Denver.

"Look who it is!" Caroline calls as we approach the outdoor hot tub situated in a common area between a few of the cabins.

We'd gone back to our room to change, the tension lingering in the form of little jolts of pleasure when Miles held the door for me and I brushed past him, or when he caught a glimpse of me changing and his eyes met mine in the mirror.

Now, we find a half dozen people already in the hot tub—including Caroline and Kevin.

I watch as Miles takes off his sweatpants. He's wearing navy shorts underneath. I keep my eyes on Miles as he leans on the edge of the tub. It barely comes up to his thigh. He's the biggest person here by far, and his sheer physical presence makes the world feel smaller.

He reaches back and pulls off his hoodie, and my breath catches. I've seen him before, but here, in the low lights from the torches, he's beautiful. Every person in that hot tub and I are invested in the way he strips down before stepping into the tub and sinking into a corner seat.

I take my time unfastening my robe and hanging it on a hook. The purple bikini shows off all my curves. From the way Miles is looking at me, I stand by my decision.

His eyes trace every inch of me with unrestrained hunger.

I start to swing a leg over the edge, and he reaches out a hand to steady me. I take it as the bubbling water slips up my calves and I drop in. The heat seeps into my body, wrapping around me like a blanket.

My bare thigh brushes Miles's shorts, my arm bumping his chest.

"Where did you two escape to earlier?" Caroline asks, cutting into my haze.

"A hot air balloon," I say as I settle into the seat next to Miles. His leg brushes mine, my shoulder leaning into his bicep. The little ripple of awareness takes this from comfy warmth to scorching heat.

Her eyes widen. "That wasn't part of the itinerary."

"Miles arranged it."

His fingers find the back of my neck, rubbing

the muscles. It's affectionate and possessive, and I relax into him.

"I've never been up in one," Caroline admits, cutting a look at Kevin next to her.

"You'd love it. Looking down on everything," Miles says, deadpan.

I stifle a laugh.

"I saw you talking with Elise outside the spa this afternoon," another sister says to me.

Caroline's face contorts. "About what?"

I stick a toe up out of the water, inspecting my pedicure. "Fashion."

The other girl giggles, and Caroline shoots her a look.

"Let's play a little game. You all know it. Anything you've done before, you have to drink."

"We're too old for this," one of the sisters complains, but Caroline lifts a hand to silence her.

"I'll go first. I've never gotten drunk enough I woke up outside."

Two sisters drink. Caroline sweeps the hot tub with her mischievous gaze.

"I've never slept with someone in this hot tub other than the person I came here with."

Kevin laughs. "The questions are supposed to rotate," he says, nudging Caroline with a shoulder.

She doesn't seem to care. "You have to drink." Her chin nods at me.

"I'm good."

My hands grip the edge of the seat underwater.

Kevin slides toward me, a slow smile on his face. "You should relax, Bee."

Miles pulls me into his lap, his arm banding around my waist. "You worry about your girl, I'll worry about mine."

Mine.

He says it as if he means it.

Honestly.

Truly.

Caroline reaches for a glass of wine resting on the ledge behind the hot tub and takes a long sip.

"Who had the biggest crush on someone in this hot tub through college? Used to trail after him and watch his basketball games every chance she got?"

Miles looks at me, curious. "That true?"

Caroline's got endless ways to try to cut me down to size. If one doesn't work, she'll try another.

"You had a crush on me back in college?" Miles murmurs against my neck.

Embarrassment rises up, adding to the heat from the water.

It's stupid to feel that way years later, but some

tiny part of me wonders if he'll think I tricked him into this weekend. Like I'm playing out some college fantasy by having my older brother's teammate on his knees for me.

"I don't..." I lift a shoulder. "Maybe a little one."

When he grabs me and turns me in his lap so I'm facing him, straddling him, there's fire in his blue eyes. His slow grin is the most genuine thing I've seen all weekend.

"Lucky me."

The words unknot something deep in my chest.

I don't feel judged or insecure.

Here with him, I'm exactly how I'm supposed to be. Who I'm supposed to be.

His hands find my ass, tugging me closer so I'm pressed against his abs, the hardness rising up against me.

Yes.

He tugs on my bikini bottoms, pulling me closer to him. His hand roams up my thigh and I inhale sharply.

More.

I grind a little against him, my lips a breath from his.

His large hands are on my waist and making their way north.

Slowly. So fucking slowly. His half-lidded gaze is intent, barely containing a need that matches mine.

When his lips brush mine, they're soft and coaxing, as if this hot tub has cast a spell on both of us.

His hands span my back, trapping my breasts against his hard chest. His cock rubs against my stomach through the thin fabric of his shorts, and he groans into my mouth.

My hand goes to his hair. I want him to touch me. To devour me.

To do whatever he fucking wants, because Miles's way has turned out far more enjoyable than the path I've been chasing this entire time.

I trace the cords of his neck with a fingertip. We're kissing as though we're the only two people in the world.

As though there's nothing else but us.

"Get a room," Caroline spits.

I'm breathing hard when Miles pulls back. His eyes are on mine. He's breathing just as hard.

"Caroline," he drawls in a deceptively pleasant voice, but he's looking at me when he says, "That's the best idea you've had all weekend."

He shifts his body, moving my hips away from him only long enough that he can stand.

Then he reaches for my hand and helps me out of the water, and I follow him without looking back.

24

BROOKE

The night air is cool on my exposed skin. I try not to catch my flip-flops on the walk back to our room, but it's hard to focus on anything but the way his hand feels threaded through mine, the tension that grows between us with every step.

"You have the key?" I ask when we pull up at the door.

Miles slips a hand in the pocket of my robe and holds up the card that glints in the light.

"Right."

He reaches past me to unlock the door. I step in first, aware of every inch of his body as I brush past him and into the room. The door clicks shut behind us.

We're alone.

There's a lamp on in the far window, probably from whoever did turndown service. Without the overhead light, it casts shadows across us and the room.

We look at each other. Miles licks his lips. I lick mine.

"Shit," he says softly, staring at me.

"You're going to tell me this is a bad idea." I stare into his eyes. "That you owe my brother or that you came to watch my back."

"Those are good reasons."

"And?"

I'm breathless before he puts his hands on my waist and pulls me to him. "And tonight, they're not good enough."

Miles kisses me. This time, he's like a starving man.

My hands stroke upward, fingers lacing around his neck so his damp hair brushes my skin. His fingers loosen the tie on my robe and brush it apart.

He groans and pulls away. We're both breathing hard.

"I want you," he whispers, sending a shiver down my spine.

"Then take me." I shove my robe off my shoulders, tossing it onto the floor. My nipples are hard, pushing against my bikini top. He grabs my waist again, pulling me toward him. His mouth goes to my neck, kissing me, his hands moving to my hair.

His body is tan and toned. I've imagined touching him the way I want to so many times. Moving my hands to his bare chest, I run my fingers over his skin, needing to feel every inch of him. He groans, the bump of his erection tenting his wet shorts.

"You wanted a fake boyfriend to impress your Kappa friends." His throat bobs as I rub him through the fabric. "How's that working out?"

"He's definitely more opinionated than I expected."

"Just wait, Princess," he promises.

He pulls off his trunks, and I bite my lip as I stare at him in awe. He's huge and thick. The idea of him inside me makes me burn up. I reach for him, wrapping my hand around him, stroking his length. He groans, head falling back in agony or pleasure or both.

If the show we were putting on outside was

provocative, what we're doing in private is hot enough to burn down the entire cabin.

But I only get in a few strokes before he pushes my hand away.

"Don't pout," he says with a smirk as he sinks to his knees.

"I'll express myself however I want."

Grabbing my bikini bottoms, he yanks them to the side.

"Feel free to do it using my name," he suggests. "Especially when I make you come."

His fingers find my clit, and his triumphant smirk has me melting even before he rubs a little circle.

I gasp. His teasing touch continues where I'm the most sensitive before drawing a lazy line back to my slit.

He's confident and unhurried, as if the only place the most popular player in the NBA would dream of being right now is between my thighs.

My fingers weave themselves into his hair. The strands are unbelievably soft, especially compared to the rest of him.

He presses a finger inside me and groans. "Would this fake boyfriend of yours tell you you're so fucking wet? That the sounds you make are such a goddamned turn-on?"

Pleasure twists tighter in my core, has me writhing against his hand. I arch against him, his face between my breasts. My nipples are hard, my skin on fire. He takes advantage, yanking down the fabric of my bikini top to bare a breast to him.

He licks the hard peak, sucking it into his mouth. The arousal is unreal. I crave more of the way he's touching me, needing me.

He pulls away and goes to the bed, pulling me with him. He grabs my knee, kissing the inside of my thigh. I moan. His hands go to my hip as he kisses down one thigh and back up the other. His hands move to my waist, pulling me to him.

"Would he tell you how much he wants to be inside you?" he whispers, his voice husky. "Because it's all I can fucking think about."

His mouth finds my wet heat, and it's wicked heaven. I grab his hair and moan. His tongue is on my clit. His hands are on my ass. Every stroke sends me higher, makes me more aware of him and us and less conscious of the world outside.

If there even is a world outside, I think hazily as pleasure rips through me.

"That's it, Princess," he murmurs against my skin.

He's holding me in place, his hands on my ass. His tongue takes over, driving me crazy.

Miles looks up at me, his eyes on mine. "Let go."

I cry out, my fist pulling on his hair. If it hurts, he doesn't let on, just locks his mouth down and keeps stroking, sucking as I explode.

Oh God.

It rips through me like a wave, utter euphoria that has every inch of my body tingling.

"You're so fucking sexy when you come." He pulls back an inch, rubbing a hand across his damp lips.

My body is still trembling from aftershocks as he unclasps my top and slides it off my shoulders. He shifts up, running his tongue over one nipple, then sucking it into his mouth. I groan, tugging on his hair. He moves to the other nipple, sucking on it.

I'm on fire. Every touch, every wet swipe of his tongue, is decadent. My eyes widen as he grabs my ass, forcing me to move against him.

His mouth finds my nipple again, sucking it into his mouth. I'm so turned on I can't think. He looks at me as he moves down my body, kissing me. "Did you think about this back in college?"

"Will you be a prick if I say yes?" I whisper.

He grins. "Absolutely."

"Yes."

I kiss him back, tasting myself on his lips.

He reaches for his bag, grabbing a condom. He drops the wrapper onto the bed, and I watch as he rolls the condom onto his hard cock.

He grabs my hips, positioning his cock at my entrance, and slides inside me. I moan, feeling every inch of him. He pulls out and slams into me again. I want more. I try to angle my hips to take him deeper.

"Fuck yes," he groans, pulling my hips back and thrusting into me. "This is the part where I'd tell you nothing I imagined feels half as good as this, as you."

He grunts, pulling back again and thrusting into me.

I can feel how close I am. My fingers are gripping his hands. He kisses my neck, then his mouth is on mine. I moan as I feel an orgasm build.

"Come on me, Princess," he whispers, kissing me.

I don't come.

I shatter.

I moan into his mouth as my stomach tightens, pleasure starting through my core and rippling through me. He rocks against me, his strokes insisting without words that I come more, longer, harder. As if this man owns my body and I'm just renting it.

Once the tingling fades a little, he pushes me onto my back and positions himself between my legs, thrusting inside me again.

"Damn," he says, his lips against mine. "You feel so good."

I feel his cock pulse and throb as he comes, his muscled body tight everywhere as he fills me.

We're both breathing hard as the feelings subside. He rolls us so we're on our sides, facing one another.

His smile fades a little, and he brushes a piece of hair from my face.

"Good thing I didn't know back then. I never would've made it back to the team, would've been too preoccupied with doing this."

I exhale hard. *It felt that way.*

There's no going back now.

But at the same time, we can't stay here forever

in the dark, where we have no responsibilities beyond each other.

"I can't believe we have to go back tomorrow," I whisper.

Miles's thumb brushes my cheek once, then again, as if he's wrestling with the same demons or his own version of them. "Not for twelve hours."

He rolls me on top.

25

MILES

The bed is too small.

I want one exactly the same size so I can sleep this close to her tomorrow, and the night after that.

The LED clock on the bedside table says it's after three. Brooke fell asleep in my arms.

I didn't come to this weekend expecting we'd land in bed.

Did I fantasize about it? Hell, yes.

But the reality blew away anything I'd imagined. How fun she was, how generous. The ways she let me touch her, the way she touched me back, how she shattered under me, with me.

The first time was a race to the bottom fueled by outright desperation. The second time and the third... it was as if I'd discovered fucking Candyland and wanted to taste every inch of it, of her, properly.

I'm not used to being around a girl I can't have for weeks, slowly driving myself crazy. Maybe there's something to be said for delayed gratification.

Finding out she had a crush on me in college should've been cute, but it meant more.

Way more.

Especially if she knew how I...

No. That's not going to help anything.

My most memorable moments in life have always been with friends. I feel the most myself surrounded by a bunch of guys on the court or in the gym or after.

But this feeling is new.

I'm nowhere near ready to go back to Denver, where I have basketball and the guys, and Brooke...

She's not mine.

My team is what matters, the basketball family I've built because my own family was light.

But she's under my skin, in my head, and until this weekend, I was searching for a way to get her out.

Now, I'm not sure I want to.

My head is buzzing.

Wait. That's my phone.

I swipe along the bedside table for it and squint to take in the number. My body's instantly on alert. Instead of hitting Decline, I get out of bed. "Hello?"

"Miles, this is the retirement home calling."

Every muscle in me goes tight.

I'm already yanking on sweatpants and heading for the door. I find shoes and slip out into the hall.

"What's wrong?" I demand once I'm outside.

The words land on me one after another.

No.

I shouldn't have left her. I should've fixed this weeks ago.

My feet tear up the carpet. "I'll be right there."

I click off, my stomach in knots.

I head back to the room.

Brooke's asleep. Her dark hair slips over her shoulders. Her mouth is swollen from mine.

"Brooke," I murmur.

She stirs but doesn't wake.

All I want to do is shift back into this bed and pull her against me.

But I can't.

Reality called and I need to fucking answer.

I grab a notepad and pen and scrawl a few sentences on it. Then I get dressed, collecting my things and leaving as quietly as I can.

26

BROOKE

Ruby: Back to the grind. Please send me good stories. The juicer the better.

I wake up alone for the second day in a row.

The difference is last night, Miles set fire to every inch of my body. We were wrapped up in one another, testing and taking until we were both too tired to keep going.

He probably went for breakfast again. The idea makes me smile.

I cross to the desk by the door, my gaze landing on a sheet of notepaper with writing on it.

I left early and didn't want to wake you.

There's a car coming for you at eleven. I'll meet you when you get back.

– M

My stomach plummets. What would have caused him to slip out in the middle of the night?

Unless he regretted that we slept together.

The ache between my thighs is a bittersweet reminder of every moment of last night.

He did what he said he'd do and acted like my boyfriend the entire weekend. In fact, he crushed the assignment.

I don't regret a moment of this weekend, and that's all that matters.

I tell myself that as I stand under the shower until my fingers and toes wrinkle.

"You missed out last night," Caroline calls when I get to breakfast at the main resort building.

She's dressed in knee-high suede boots, a thick

sweater draped intentionally revealing one shoulder. Her pale hair falls in relaxed curls, but her eyes are red as if she didn't sleep.

"Kevin and I are engaged." She holds up her hand, hoisting a massive sparkling diamond in the air like a weapon.

It does deliver a gut punch.

Not because I want anything with Kevin, but seeing him commit to her when he broke up with me for covering for him manages to scald some portion of my soul that I thought was safe.

"Elise," she says, and I realize that the woman is right behind us. "I didn't mean for you to overhear."

"Not at all, it's wonderful news." Elise's eyes brighten with genuine pleasure.

"Isn't it? Someone's follower count always goes up following their engagement and wedding planning. It would be great exposure for your brand."

There's no way Caroline orchestrated this engagement for the purposes of impressing Elise.

Is there?

Even I'm not so cynical as to think she's been plotting this for weeks—longer.

But... what if Caroline's stock was slipping and she took drastic measures to address the fall?

Elise smiles. "I appreciate that, but I've made my decision. I'm going with someone different."

Caroline smiles in a way that doesn't look like she was rejected. "Different can be good. It can also cause problems if it doesn't align with your brand. Is this what you're looking for?"

She holds out her phone, showing Elise.

Elise's nostrils flare delicately.

I extend my hand, and the other woman passes me the device.

The photo is dark and blurry, but it's definitely me straddling Miles in the hot tub. His fingers dig into my waist, my hand grips his shoulder. If you can't see his face, the bear tattoo makes it pretty clear.

Except it's not a photo. It's a video.

Me kissing Miles, my body pressed to his. Though the water obscures half of what we're doing, the water licks at my back in rhythm with our movements.

"It looks to me as if that moment was intended to be private," Elise says at last.

Gratitude wells up.

"Excuse us, Elise." I grab Caroline's arm and drag her down the hall.

"What the hell?" I toss when I round to face her.

"Some of us have worked all our lives for our image. You go around saying and doing whatever you want and still get your way."

"You can't believe that." I stare at her, incredulous.

"It's true. You fucked up in school and came out unscathed. I guess your boyfriend is perfect for you."

I laugh. It's the only possible reaction to her words. "I genuinely have no idea what you're talking about."

"Miles Garrett put Kevin in the hospital the summer after junior year."

My mouth falls open in shock. It's so unhinged, but I have to give her credit. Just when I think she can't go any lower, she does.

"Miles was in the NBA, Caroline. Your math doesn't add up."

"It was April, right before exams, and he was in town for an alumni event. I have proof. These are the photos from that night." She pulls up pictures of Kevin, his face swollen and purple.

My stomach twists with nausea. Whatever did happen to Kevin, it doesn't look made up.

I never saw this, which means it must have happened after he broke up with me.

And it couldn't possibly have anything to do with Miles.

"Miles is a professional athlete. He's one of the most popular players in the entire league," I say.

"I'm guessing he didn't tell you."

Nothing is adding up. I hate being blindsided in front of Caroline, but I have to believe this is one more ploy to knock me off guard.

"Why would he do that?" I demand.

Caroline flicks her hair out of her face, the diamond dancing in the light. "You'll have to ask him."

Nova: So I've been sending you good vibes for your pitch. And secretly praying you and Miles would hook up (don't hate me). Can't wait to hear the details when you get home! :)

The scenery passes slowly on the two-hour drive in the back of the limo that arrived as Miles said it would, but my head is spinning.

My text convo with Miles hasn't been touched since before the reunion. His social has been silent too.

His note is in my pocket, and I run my fingers over it.

Caroline's accusation is nuts.

Except...

The night she claims this happened was right around the time Kevin broke up with me.

I didn't see him all summer after that, so I wouldn't have known.

I type out a text to Miles, but I don't know how to ask the question.

Did you hit Kevin back in college? Did you put him in the hospital?

If it's the truth, Miles has been hiding it for a long time.

More than that, if he hurt Kevin when he was a rookie in the league, that could have repercussions for his career.

Why on earth did he do it?

The questions won't leave my mind. They spin

and twist in my brain right up until the car pulls up to my building.

We'll figure this out, I tell myself.

Miles said he'd meet me once I got back.

Someone opens the door...

But it's not Miles.

"What are you doing here?" I demand when I recognize the man blocking my way out.

Jay stares at me with the kind of look he'd have when I fell into a ditch and scraped my knee as a kid—the look that says I'm in big trouble.

"We need to talk."

Thank you for reading *Hard to Fake*!

Miles and Brooke's swoony, emotional, sexy story continues in ***Hard to Take***.

For writing updates, early excerpts and exclusive giveaways...

Join my VIP List and never miss a thing!

www.piperlawsonbooks.com/subscribe

ACKNOWLEDGMENTS

Thank you for reading Hard to Fake! I loved coming back to the Kodiaks, and Brooke and Miles are the perfect narrators for what's coming next.

This story wouldn't have happened without the support of my awesome readers, including my ARC readers. Thank you for providing endless enthusiasm, cheerleading, early feedback, and help spreading the word.

Becca Mysoor: It blows my mind how many good ideas you have on the regular. Thank you for being such an inspiration and overall smart cookie.

Cassie Robertson: I'm amazed you still let me slide into your calendar after all these years. Someday, I'll write a scene with blocking on the first pass. (Fine, the second.)

Dria Roland: Your expertise, empathy and

enthusiasm made this story so much better. I am already obsessed with you.

Devon Burke: I hate the thought of writing a book without having you to catch my typos and show biz faux pas. (Is that how you write that? I'm adding this note after you read the book, so we'll never know.)

Annette Brignac: You are the first person with a stunning mockup for cover reveal day and a paper bag for hyperventilating on "why the hell did I decide to write this book?!" day. I am in awe of you.

Kate Tilton: You do the things I should be doing, and you do them better than I would. Thank you for making my life better.

Lori Jackson and Emily Wittig: You take my random ideas and wacky gradients and making art from them. Thank you for responding to my emails when I ask for one more tweak three months after you've forgotten who I am.

Georgana Grinstead, Kim, Christina, Sarah, and the entire VPR team: You make the complicated work of publishing seem effortless. Thank you for your wisdom, genius, and tireless effort to help readers find books they'll love.

Last but not least, thank YOU for reading. Truly. Knowing we're living in these words and worlds together is the best part of any gig I've ever had.

Love always,

Piper

KING OF THE COURT SERIES

After being dumped and losing my job the same week, the last thing my broken heart needs is a rebound.

A steamy, grumpy sunshine sports romance featuring a woman down on her luck, a star basketball player with a filthy mouth, and a connection neither of them can deny.

OFF-LIMITS SERIES

Turns out the beautiful man from the club is my new professor... But he wasn't when he kissed me.

Off-Limits is a forbidden age gap college romance series. Find out what happens when the beautiful man from the club is Olivia's hot new professor.

WICKED SERIES

Rockstars don't chase college students. But Jax Jamieson never followed the rules.

Wicked is a new adult rock star series full of nerdy girls, hot rock stars, pet skunks, and ensemble casts you'll want to be friends with forever.

RIVALS SERIES

At seventeen, I offered Tyler Adams my home, my life, my heart. He stole them all.

Rivals is an angsty new adult series. Fans of forbidden romance, enemies to lovers, friends to lovers, and rock star romance will love these books.

ENEMIES SERIES

I sold my soul to a man I hate. Now, he owns me.

Enemies is an enthralling, explosive romance about an American DJ and a British billionaire. If you like wealthy, royal alpha males, enemies to lovers, travel or sexy romance, this series is for you!

TRAVESTY SERIES

My best friend's brother grew up. Hot.

Travesty is a steamy romance series following best friends who start a fashion label from NYC to LA. It contains best friends brother, second chances, enemies to lovers, opposites attract and friends to lovers stories. If you like sexy, sassy romances, you'll love this series.

PLAY SERIES

I know what I want. It's not Max Donovan. To hell with his money, his gaming empire, and his joystick.

Play is an addictive series of standalone romances with slow burn tension, delicious banter, office romance and unforgettable characters. If you like smart, quirky, steamy enemies-to-lovers, contemporary romance, you'll love Play.

MODERN ROMANCE SERIES

When your rich, handsome best friend asks you to be his fake girlfriend? Say no.

Modern Romance is a smart, sexy series of contemporary romances following a set of female friends running a relationship marketing company in NYC. If you enjoy hot guys who treat their families like gold, fun antics, dirty talk, real characters, steamy scenes, badass heroines and smart banter, you'll love the Modern Romance series.

ABOUT THE AUTHOR

Piper Lawson is a WSJ and USA Today bestselling author of smart and steamy romance.

She writes women who follow their dreams, best friends who know your dirty secrets and love you anyway, and complex heroes you'll fall hard for.

Piper lives in Canada with her tall and brilliant husband. She's a sucker for dark eyes, dark coffee, and dark chocolate.

For a complete reading list, visit
www.piperlawsonbooks.com/books

**Subscribe to Piper's VIP email list
www.piperlawsonbooks.com/subscribe**

amazon.com/author/piperlawson

bookbub.com/authors/piper-lawson

instagram.com/piperlawsonbooks

facebook.com/piperlawsonbooks

goodreads.com/piperlawson